LOVE AND HENNESSY: 4

AN ADDICTIVE KIND OF LOVE

Carmen Lashay

Text **Treasured** to **444999**
To subscribe to our Mailing
List.
Interested in becoming a part
of the Treasured Publications
family?
Submit manuscripts to
Info@Treasuredpub.com

AUTHOR'S
ACKNOWLEDGEMENTS

First and foremost, I want to take time out to give thanks to God who is forever the head of my life. With him, all things are possible. I am so very thankful and blessed to be bringing you all my 10th book, and I'm so excited about that fact. As many of you know, this series is my baby, so although it was fun to write, it also took me awhile because I sadly did not want to bring it to a close. Ghost is bae all day, so I can admit I cried when I wrote "the end." I'm very excited to share it with all of you though. I also want to take a few moments and give thanks to a few people who I love, admire, and that hold a special place in my heart. They go above and beyond to make this journey I'm walking an easy one for me with just the support they display. To my parents whom I love dearly, I want to thank you for just loving me and raising such a strong-willed, and motivated young lady. To my wonderful husband who is always my #1 fan thank you for encouraging me daily to reach for the sky's in my pursuit of my dreams. To my sister Paulesha Hill, I thank you for staying on me when I want to give up, and motivating me to keep pushing forward. I also thank you for always encouraging me to keep going when I start to doubt myself. To my long time best friend Keiaira Cooper who is always there for me no matter what time it is, you are always ready for me to bounce ideas off you and offer me your honest constructive criticism. You understand I don't always need a yes man rather someone to tell me if that doesn't sound right. You always read each and every book I write and put up with me during my meltdown moments. Our sessions always give me a burst of energy and motivation. To the best publisher that any girl could ever have, the fabulous Treasure Malian, I thank you from the bottom of my heart. I could write a full book, and still couldn't say thank you enough. I'm everything that I am because you decided to take a chance on me. You stay onto me like white on rice lol, but it's appreciated because it forces me out of my comfort zone, and to heights I never imagined I could go to. I'm eternally grateful. To my pen sisters of Treasured Publications, I love each and everyone of you ladies, and I'm so very proud of you guys. All for one, and one for all, may we continue reaching for the stars together in this new year. To my entire Miller and Smith family, I love you all so very much and just know I'm doing this for you guys. Last, but certainly not least, I want to personally thank you, the readers. Without your continued support none of this would be possible. I thank each and everyone of you who took the time to read my books, whether you purchased it, or borrowed it, I still thank you. As always you can follow me on the social media links below, and be sure to leave me a review on Amazon, I do enjoy reading them; they are the highlight of my day. Without further ado, I give you the long anticipated finale,

LOVE AND HENNESSY 4.

@JASMINE MILLER-SMITH – FACEBOOK PERSONAL PAGE

@AUTHOR CARMEN LASHAY- FACEBOOK AUTHOR PAGE

@AUTHORESSCARMEN LASHAY – FACEBOOK AUTHOR READERS PAGE WHERE I TYPICALLY DROP RELEASE DATES AND SNEAK PEAKS

@PARDON_MY_PRETTI_ - INSTAGRAM PAGE

@MARRIED&BOUGIE – SNAPCHAT

IN LOVING MEMORY OF MY COUSIN, WILLISHA "LISHA" MILLER. GONE BUT NEVER FORGOTTEN. MAY YOUR SOUL FIND PEACE IN HEAVEN WITH GRANNY.

PROLOGUE

GHOST

"Yo' ass is rude," I said to Tommie.

"That's you on the phone wit' folks. You keep accepting phone calls, but you told me that it was my day, and I had you all to myself," Tommie said, pouting. We had been out shopping for the new house, all day. Since the incident with the plastic lips, I moved my family to a more secure location similar to Menace's house. Complete with guards at the gate, and stationed around the premises. I also hired body guards to always escort Tommie and Royalty around. Even though I had eliminated the only threat that I had, I still wasn't taking any chances. Matthew got back to me and said the CI had disappeared, so shit, a nigga was stress free from the hells of the streets, and was focused on trying to get me a Jr. If Jasmine and Dom had a boy, and I didn't get my Jr, I was gone be mad as hell.

"I'm hungry," Tommie said.

"Cool, we can hit Pappadeux. A nigga got a taste for some seafood."

Pulling into the restaurant, we went inside and ordered our food.

"So, I was thinking…" Tommie said after our drinks were brought to the table. "It's time you made good on that promise you told me that I could fill the position at the clothing store." *Shit, I forgot I even told her ass that shit.*

"We can discuss it later," I said.

"No, this is later from the first discussion."

"You not gone let this go, are you?"

"No," she said taking a sip of her Cat-30 Hurricane.

"Okay, fine. First thing Monday morning, you can start your training."

"Training?"

"You fine and all shawty, but everything that comes through my spot goes to training first," I said laughing.

"I can do that," she said just happy that I was letting her work.

"Now let's eat so we can get out of here. I know you gone have me running all day tomorrow even though I done paid these folks to do that," I said because she suckered me into dishing out 15 thousand for an engagement dinner party, just to announce the damn engagement like we couldn't simply call folks on the phone and tell them. I paid for caterers, a party planner, and decorators, yet my ass was still running all over New York anyway, getting stuff together. I should have included my damn self in all the money I was shelling out.

"Don't be like that. You only get married once, and you told me I could have whatever I like, and budgets are for suckers."

"Damn, I did say that," I said, laughing. "Well hell, that was before I realized a simple dinner cost 15 thousand dollars. I don't understand why the dinner couldn't be the wedding. I don't need fancy shit. I just need you and Royalty and Landon Carter Jr," I said.

"Nice try," Tommie said laughing. The joke was on her though because a nigga damn sure hadn't been pulling out. I wanted a football field full of kids, so if it wasn't my Jr this go around, we would just keep trying until we got his ass.

Leaving out the restaurant, a nigga was lit as fuck. Shit I tried some type of swamp drink, and was sleeping on that bitch. I thought it wasn't strong, so I drank two, now I felt like I was floating.

"Babe, you drunk," Tommie said laughing as she held onto me for balance as we walked towards the car.

"Naw shawty, a nigga lit, but I ain't drunk. Yo little ass on the other hand is light weight. Shit you can barely stand up." I told her as she stopped walking and stared dancing.

"Throw that ass in a circle." I couldn't do anything but shake my head at her, but when she came and stood directly in front of me throwing that ass all over me, my dick instantly sprang to life. I never had a problem with Tommie's weight. I've always told her that she was beautiful just the way that she was, baby weight and all. She insisted to hit the gym hard after she had Royalty though and now, she was so fucking fine that I told her she better not go back to that gym for a long time. I didn't need her losing not another pound. I loved her either way, big or small. However, her body right now just did something to me. I'm surprised her ass wasn't pregnant now, just by how I had to bend her ass over every time I saw her. She turned me on in anything she wore these days. That's how bad she was. From that tiny ass waist line, to those super thick ass thighs, to the delicious melons that sat up just right, my wife had a body most women paid lots of money for.

"Tommie, girl, gon' head and come get in this car," I warned her, hitting the locks to my Ashton Martin. I had to pull out one of my toys for date night tonight. Completely ignoring me, she turned to face me as she started kissing down my neck. That was one of my hot spots, so I grabbed her by her ass, cupped it firmly, and pulled her towards me. We had about a 5 minute make out session, consisting of kissing and licking on exposed parts until I broke away from her, and told her to get inside the car. When I walked around and hopped in the drives side, she had hiked her dress up, revealing the fact that she wasn't wearing any panties.

"Bruh, you testing a nigga right now," I said licking my lips as I stared hungrily at her pretty pink, shaved, pussy. That shit was my weakness. Starting the car up, Tank's *Fucking With Me* came blasting through the radio.

"Baby this is our song. Remember this was playing the first time you saw me naked in Jasmine's kitchen," she said, singing off key.

"Bout to eat it up for a while, let me through." I sang to her. Only Tommie knew that a nigga could actually sing, and we were gonna keep it that way. Slapping her hand out the way, I dove head first inside of her shit right there in the parking lot. A nigga was slurping and sucking on her pearl for dear life.

"Quit screaming so loud, they gone think a nigga in here murdering your ass," I said laughing because her drunk ass was louder than usual.

"I can't help it. Oh my God," she moaned. After about 5 minutes, I sat up, and kissed her in the mouth letting her see how good she tasted. Shit was the best thing I've ever tasted.

"I love you, my wife," I said kissing her again. Every since I had put that ring on her finger, I had been calling her my wife because a far as I was concerned, she was, and a piece of paper wouldn't change anything only solidify it. Throwing the car in drive, I pulled drove out of the parking lot headed to the house. Reaching over, Tommie started unbuckling and unzipping my pants. I kept my eyes on the road as she pulled my erect penis out and started jacking it up and down. The shit felt so good, that I caught myself closing my eyes a few times.

"Fuck girl," I said as she put my dick in my mouth making it disappear down her throat. "Fuck baby, wait until we get home. Shit, I'ma wreck this bitch," I said, swerving for a second time.

"No I want it now," she said.

"Daddy gon' take care of that when we get home."

"Naw, daddy is gonna take care of this now." Tommie said as she climbed onto my lap reverse cowgirl style, and slid down onto my waiting dick. Biting down on my lip until I tasted blood, I tried not to scream out like a little bitch, but that's how good the shit felt.

"I'll steer, you work the gas pedals," she said squeezing her walls around my dick. Saying fuck it, I grabbed her by the waist, and started slamming into her over and over again working her from the bottom as she worked me from the top.

"You gon' have my son?" I asked. reaching my hand around and grabbed her throat. Nodding her head in a yes response, I said,

"Use your words, let me hear that shit."

"Yes baby, I'ma have your son, fuck. I'll have your son, another daughter, shit, twins…" she moaned as she started bouncing up and down on my dick.

"Ahhh God, hmmm," she said. "Baby I'm bout to cum."

"Me to, keep your eyes on the road baby," I said as I felt that nut in my toes. Holding onto her tightly, I came so deep inside of her, I thought I touched her soul. Pulling up to another red light, she hopped off of my lap and back inside of her seat.

"Girl, you wild as hell. Freaky ass."

"You like it though," she said, sticking her tongue out.

" Shit, you almost got us killed."

"But did we die though?" She laughed just as a car came slamming into us from my side pushing us into another lane. Everything was blurry as I tried to sit up.

"Tommie," I said, shaking my head trying to stay awake. I saw her out the corner of my eyes slumped over the seat. "Baby," I said as my car door was flung open. Reaching for my gun blindly, I was too late as I heard,

"When you try and kill somebody, make sure they are dead bitch," before gun shots rang out

POW! POW! POW!

And then everything went dark.

CHAPTER 1

"LORD, PLEASE DON'T DO THIS TO ME..."

TOMMIE

Everything happened so fast as I felt the hard hit from behind us, causing me to hit my head hard against the dashboard. The impact of the blow caused me to be temporarily unconscious, but when I came to, I heard muffled voices to my left followed by gunshots ringing out. Tears swelled up in my eyes because I didn't know if Landon was the one shot or not, as I remained in the same position, refusing to move and praying he was okay. But, if he wasn't shot, wouldn't he be talking to me? My heart began to pound rapidly as if it were going to burst out of my chest as silence consumed the car. *Landon, I hope you are okay*, I thought to myself. Not wanting to look over at the driver side because I was afraid of what I'd see, with my head still down, I reached around until my hands landed onto my purse. I had purchased a gun a few weeks back, and kept it in my purse at all times. Gripping the gun tightly in my hands, I tried to calm my nerves as I heard someone trying to open my door which appeared to be jammed. *Shit they came back to finish the job off.* I screamed in my head. If Landon was down, it was left up to me to protect my husband until I could get us to safety. Cocking the clip back on the gun, I said

"You can do this Tommie," I whispered to myself as I felt the cold night air kissing my skin as the door was pried open at the same time as I sat up pointing the gun in the direction of the intruder. With my eyes closed so tightly, I blindly let off three shots.

"Whoa ma'am, I'm only here to help you. I stopped to see if you guys were okay," a guy said to me. Opening my eyes, I saw him getting up with his hands in the air. I guess he had dove for cover when I started shooting.

"Who are you?" I asked. My hands were shaking, and my vision was a little blurred. "Landon, you okay?" I said over my shoulder, not taking my eyes off of the man.

"My wife and I saw the wrecked car and stopped to see if you guys needed help ma'am," he said, visibly shaking. At this point, I didn't know whether to believe him or not. *"Trust nothing you see and everything you feel,"* Landon's voice rang into my head saying. My instinct was telling me he was being honest with me, but at this point, I couldn't be sure of anything.

"Baby, are they okay?' I heard a voice say as a woman came into view. Gun still raised, I turned it on her this time as I called out to Landon again.

"Whoa ma'am , it's no need for that," he said immediately going into protection mode as he stood in front of his wife. Hands shaking, not knowing if I should trust my gut telling me they were here to help or not, my head begin to spin, as I felt blood dripping into my eyes. Wiping my face, I lowered the gun and looked around the car as my eyes landed onto Landon slumped over the steering wheel.

"Landon," I screamed throwing the gun down, as I leaned over to his side. Feeling restrained, I unsnapped the seatbelt from around my body allowing me better access to get to him.

"Call for help!" I yelled as blood pool formed in his seat. Not wanting to move him, I searching rapidly over his body trying to find the source of the blood, I just didn't know where he was hit at.

"Baby, call the police," the guy said to his wife.

"Don't you die on me, Landon. You hear me Ghost, you fucking hear me, don't you die on me. Royalty needs you. I-I-I need you Landon," I choked up as I shook my head, trying to stay focused. Ever since I sat up, my head had been pounding out of control.

****

BOOM!

The paramedics rushed through the double doors of the emergency room , rushing Landon in as I ran beside the gurney with tears pouring down my face as I looked at the love of my life, my king, laying there still.

"Ma'am , you can't go back here," a nurse said to me once we came to another set of doors.

"You need to get checked out yourself ma'am. That cut on your head looks deep. You might need stitches," another nurse said to me.

"No, I have to go with him, I have to go with him," I refused, hysterically.

"We will keep you updated. Right now, you are no good to him if you don't get that cut looked at. It looks to me like you've lost a considerable amount of blood yourself." The nurse said.

"I'm fine, I'm going with him. He needs me. Y'all got me fucked up. Try and stop me, and I'm shutting this entire ER the fuck down," I yelled meaning every word of what I was saying. I was on ten at this point and anybody could get it. I was delirious and very hysterical, and all I wanted was Landon.

"Ma'am, I understand your frustration, concerns and anger, but please, you have to calm down and allow us to do our job. What good are you to him if you in jail when he needs you to most? Let the doctors help him baby. He gone be alright. When he comes out of surgery I will come and get you. Now come on and get yourself looked at baby. You not looking well yourself," an older black nurse said to me as the others went behind double doors that I was currently not being allowed to go into. Finally agreeing with them, I allowed myself to be led in a daze to a room of my own as they patched me up, took blood from me, and stitched my wounds. I had to have eight stitches and as much as I hate getting them, I stared into space the entire time displaying very little emotion. My body had completely shut down, and I couldn't even function properly.

"Did you know that you are pregnant?" The older black nurse who I now know was named Nurse Betty said to me.

"Pregnant?" I repeated as I the word was very foreign to me. Looking down at the chart, she said, "Yes according to the charts, you are about 6 weeks along. You are severely dehydrated, so we are going to start you on some fluids."

"Pregnant" I again repeated to myself thinking back to how Landon has been trying since Royalty was born, to have a son.

"You can't leave us now, Landon. Your son is about to come," I said to no one in particular.

"Baby, is there someone I can call for you?" Nurse Betty said to me. Nodding my head, I gave her Jasmine's number.

"When will I know something?" I asked, barely above a whisper as she started me on my IV.

"I honestly do not know," she said to me finishing up and preparing to leave. "You just focus on getting some rest, baby. Your body needs it or that baby you have inside of you won't have a fighting chance," she said as she walked out of the room with her clipboard in hand and sorrow in her eyes. Laying back on the bed, I balled up into a fetal position and just begin to rock back and forth as I prayed to myself. I just knew this was a cruel joke, a nightmare of some sort that I would wake up from at any minute and Landon would be laying beside me, snoring extra loudly. Laughing to myself at how horrible he sounds when he is sleep, I couldn't help the tears that followed. I went from a weak and broken person who loved a man who didn't love her back, a person who took more ass whoopings than she gave out all in the name of love, to a strong confident woman who was loved unconditionally by a hell of a man. A man who not only loved all of me, but my daughter, as well. A man who if you even looked at me or Royalty wrong, he was going off. A man who would never allow anyone to disrespect me and would never do it himself. A man who would lay his life down for his family. That was the type of man I had in Landon. His love for me was rare, something that only came once in a lifetime, and I didn't know what I would do if I ever lost that love. How I would go on for my baby. Crying and rocking myself for a bit longer, I slowly drifted off to sleep as the effects of the medicine finally kicked in.

***

POW! POW! POW! BOOM!

Flashbacks of the wreck and gun shots, and of Landon being slumped over caused me to awake from my sleep in a fit of screams shaking with sweat pouring from my body. Looking around wildly, reality set in that it wasn't all a dream, and it had really happened.

"Please God, Please don't take him away from me. It isn't his time yet, he isn't done here on earth yet," I cried as the door to my room opened and Nurse Betty walked in.

"Hush that crying, chile. It's going to be okay, just give it to the Lord. That's a strong young man down there and he is fighting for his life. You need to fight with him," she said to me.

"I have to get out of this bed. I need to get my baby, and I can't just lay around here doing nothing," I cried.

"You was discharged awhile ago. I just needed you to get some rest," she said to me. Hearing this, I jumped up tossing the covers off of me and began to scramble to grab my things.

"Remember something baby, a man may be the protector of the house, but you are the glue that holds your family together. You need to be his glue right now," she said to me. Pausing for a moment to process what she said to me, I rushed past her down the hallway and towards the front desk to ask them about Landon.

"Ma'am, a doctor will be with you shortly. That's all I can disclose at this time." the front desk nurse said. Catching myself before I went off on her, I bit my tongue as I walked off towards the bathroom. I planned on calling Jasmine and Dom after I finished because the nurse probably didn't get through to them or something. Once I was finished handling my business, I walked out the bathroom and was headed towards to find a payphone since I didn't have my cell when I spotted Jasmine and Dom in the waiting area. Walking over to them, Jasmine met me halfway.

"Tommie, are you okay?" she said dramatically as she ran to me.

"What happened?" Dom barked.

"I-I-, I don't know." I began to stammer, already feeling overwhelmed

"What the fuck you mean, you don't know?"

"I don't know Dominic, One minute we were laughing, next minute something slammed into us. It happened so fast," I cried.

"Don't be fucking yelling at her," Jasmine said to him coming to my defense.

"Fuck," he said punching the wall. Walking back over to where they was sitting at, I ran down everything from last night not leaving anything out including our steamy sex episode. I included details of everything down to me hopping off of his dick, us laughing, and someone slamming into us.

"Something is just not adding up. Bro stayed on me about not getting caught out here without my vest on, so I'm tryna see how he didn't have his. Shit not making no sense. Unless when y'all was fucking, you took it off him?" He said eyeballing me.

"I don't know. I may have and don't remember. We was drunk and fucking, who asks what they can and can't take off?" I said.

"Shit, somebody who knows the streets hot and knows that without it, niggas can catch my mans slipping. I'm saying though the vest ain't have nothing to do with you getting the dick. So what you take it off for?" He spat.

"That's enough Dominic, you got my sister real life fucked up," Jasmine yelled.

"Shit I done hit plenty of hoes in the car with a vest on and ain't nan bitch tried to take it off a nigga to get this dick because it don't stand in the way. Who gets fully undressed to fuck in the car?" He said ignoring Jasmine as he continued going off with his accusations.

"But maybe you secretly felt some type of way about him killing your weak ass baby daddy. I mean you was with dude almost ten years, and put up with him beating your ass that whole time and still loved dude. But, you leave him for a few months, and all of a sudden dude on your shit list? A nigga is not buying it. Your ass prolly was waiting for the right time to strike," he yelled, his fists balled up.

"You son of a bitch. I know like hell you not sitting here accusing my sister of setting Ghost up. You wrong as fuck," Jasmine said.

"Am I J? How long you know Ghost? How many times a nigga caught him slipping like this? This the most observant nigga I know. He peep shit long before the shit even happen so what happened different this time? Shit not adding up. Yo on some real shit, y'all got me so fucked up right now," he said shaking his head as tears he was desperately trying to hold rolled down his eyes. At this point he didn't even bother wiping them away. While Jas tried consoling him, I jumped up breaking my silence. I had let him get it all out, but now he was going to hear me.

"Nigga, let me tell you one muthafuckin' thing. That nigga that's laid up in that hospital bed, the one you call your friend, I would die for him in a heartbeat. If I could have, I would have taken all of them bullets. You say how can I stop loving somebody after ten years? Shit it wasn't hard when I had somebody like Landon showing me daily what real love actually was. Rodney was all I had known since I first discovered boys. Everything I knew about boys love and sex, I learned from him. It took a real man stepping in showing me the correct way for me to realize how wrong I had been for years. Shit I thought getting choked was the way you love somebody, but Landon taught me that's what you do to your woman when you fucking her not loving her. I thought all niggas cheat, and it was okay, as long as he knew where home was at. But, that was before Landon showed me that if you love someone you won't even think twice about another bitch. You make your girl laugh at these bitches, not these bitches laugh at your girl. I love that man with everything in me and the only thing I was mad at concerning the Rodney situation, was me not being able to pull the trigger myself. You got me fucked up, if you think I don't love Landon Carter, and I'm not hurt to my soul that he's hurt. I'm trying to be strong for both my kids and my man," I said as I sat down in a chair with my head bent down resting on my legs as I prayed harder than I've ever prayed before.

"Both your kids?" Jasmine said catching that last part. Getting up, I walked away from them.

"Aye, Tommie, man… a nigga sorry, okay? And I ain't never apologized to nobody, but I'm sorry. Shit that's my mans, through and through. I'm just going through it," Dom said to me. The apology sounded fucked up, but I know Dom, so I know it was sincere. Still, I kept walking.

"Tommie, don't go," Jasmine said.

"Yeah, I'm not letting you out of me sight. Ghost ain't about to kill me cause something happened to his shawty and son," Dom said which paused me and caused me to turn around with tears in my eyes. "Girl quit all that mushy shit… you know that's my nigga's Jr. or you better pray it is.

Cause if it isn't, you know y'all trying again and again. So you just better get on this big train," he said laughing as we joined in because he was right. If I had another girl, Landon ass would have me barefoot and pregnant again before my six weeks were even up. He wouldn't care if it took him nine tries, he was getting his Jr.

***

A few hours later, we were still sitting around the waiting room, waiting on a doctor to come tell us something regarding Landon. Rocking Royalty in my arms, I adjusted her weight as I moved my leg onto the floor. I had been sitting on it, and now it was going to sleep. Glancing down at my baby, I couldn't help but to laugh at how she was currently knocked out like she had really just worked a sixteen hour shift. My baby had her arms really thrown all crazy stretched out on me. Even with headphones on blocking out the sound, I just knew she was snoring loudly. For her not to be Landon's biological daughter, she mimicked him in every way possible even down to the way she snored. Not being able to look away, I just stared at my baby sleeping peacefully, without a care in the world. I had Mariah to bring her to me, at the hospital because I wanted her here with me and her father.

"At this moment with my arms outstretched

I need you to make a way as you have done so many times before"

As Smokey Norfolk's *"I Need You Now"* blasted on repeat in my ear, I was still sitting in the same spot. Against Jasmine's wishes, I hadn't went home to change clothes, or eaten anything. I wanted Landon, and I wasn't moving until somebody took me to him.

"Here, give me my niece," Jasmine said stretching her arms out to take Royalty from me. Clutching her tighter, I shook my head no.

"Come on sis, let Jas take her. Go get yourself cleaned up. It's dried up blood on your clothes. You really want baby girl seeing you like that? She been sleep the whole time which is good, but you want her waking up and seeing her mother with her hair thrown over her head looking like who shot John and forgot to kill him? Clothes all beat up, looking like a bum?" Dom said.

"You didn't have to say all that, damn. You a rude ass nigga," Jasmine said to him.

"Aye, at least a nigga honest though."

"Well, yeah. True, I agree with that," Jasmine said.

"Thanks for having my back," I said, sarcastically to her.

"I do have your back baby, that's why I'm trying to get my niece while you go get yourself together," Jasmine said.

"Family of Landon Carter?" I heard as I jumped up swiftly handing Royalty to Mariah as I power walked over to the doctor.

"What's the status, doctor?" Dom asked, getting straight to the point. The doctor paused before he answered him, but the look he gave said it all.

"Noooooooooo!!!" I screamed before I passed out.

CHAPTER 2

"SHIT GETTING CRAZY OUT HERE…."

GHOST

BEEP!BEEP!

Hearing noises, I slowly opened my eyes to a dark room, a banging ass headache, and my body on fire. Feeling a stinging feeling on the side of my neck, I groaned as I reached my hand up to the burning spot but, instead of feeling my neck, I was instead met with bondages.
What the hell happened?" I thought to myself, but unable to remember. Fully opening my eyes, I noticed the beige ceiling were not what I was used to seeing first thing in the morning. I know like hell I ain't get drunk and pass out some damn where.

"This got Dom name written all over it. Tommie gon' kill my ass. Fuck!" I said to myself.

BEEP!BEEP!

"Yo, what the fuck is that annoying ass sound?" I said to no one in particular as I turned my head to my right. That's when I noticed the IV machine, as well as the heart and blood pressure monitor. *What the fuck?* Just then, the door opened and in walked a nurse.

"Say what the fuck am I doing here?" I yelled at her. However, instead of the bitch answering me, she went about her business checking her chart, and the machines.

"Yo, is yo bald headed ass deaf or something, bruh? I asked you what the fuck I'm doing here? Dead ass, bruh." I asked, feeling myself getting angrier by the second. I wish I could go to sleep and restart this damn day. Nigga did not expect to wake up to this shit. Where the hell was Tommie, and why wasn't she here?

"Even though you all banged up after having been shot multiple times, you still fine as fuck. I gave you a sponge bath before I dressed you in your gown and lawd, I almost swallowed your dick inch by inch. I even went into the bathroom and got myself off just thinking about that big dick," The nurse said to me with her back turned as she laughed at her own remark.

"Word? Shit under different circumstances, a nigga wouldn't have even objected to that offer but this good dick belongs to Tommie, baby girl. Besides yo ugly ass need to swallow some fucking edge control, now again what the fuck isgoing on? When was I shot? Where?" I said in frustration as I pushed the call button onto the floor causing her to jump and turn around quickly.

"Mr. Carter, you're awake?" She said, shocked.

"Of course I'm awake. Nigga been awake this entire time. Heard all that nasty shit You was talking about, too. Your ass better not let my girl hear you saying that shit either, bruh," I said but for the first time, I noticed that I didn't actually hear my voice. How the fuck I'm saying shit then? Blinking rapidly, I looked wildly around the room as everything begin to spin.

"What the fuck is going on?" I screamed inside of my head as the machines begin going off all at once.

"Mr. Carter, I'm going to need you to calm down. The nurse said as more people rushed into the room.

"Fuck y'all," I said, but once again, they did not hear me. Cursing to myself, I tried with all of my might to get out of the bed. Willing myself to move, I looked over and noticed the baldheaded hoe from earlier grabbing my IV shooting some medicine inside of it. Getting a good look at her name tag, I memorized it inside of my head as my eyes become heavy. I was most definitely killing that hoe when I got out of this shit, and that was my last thought before I closed my eyes and succumbed to the effects of the medicine.

***

Opening my eyes again, I noticed that this time it was dark in the room when I woke up. Feeling a little better this go around, I tried for five minutes to sit up in the bed until I finally managed to pull myself up. Next, I was determined to get out of the bed. Earlier, a nigga lost track of time, but ol girl said I came in shot up and shit. If that's true, then where the hell was Dom, or Tommie at? I know they along with Jasmine would definitely have been up here by now. Some shit was going on, and a nigga most definitely wasn't about to lay around while my family was in danger. Naw, banged up and all, I was ready for whatever. It was gon' take more than some bullets to put a real nigga down. As I begin snatching all the cords off me including the damn IV, those machines once again begin going off. All the commotion must have alerted nurses, because as soon as I'd gotten all the cords off me, one burst into the room.

"Mr. Carter, are you okay? What are you doing sir?" The nurse asked me frantically, as she rushed over to my bed attempting to hook the cords back up. This nurse was a different one than the hoe from earlier which I was grateful for on one end, but annoyed with on the other. They obviously didn't know who the fuck a nigga was if they thought I was about to be chilling in this damn bed like shit was all good. Ignoring her, I begin to focus on the task of getting out of this bed as I started feeling pressure inside of my throat. Grabbing at my throat, I felt the cord for the first time coming out of it. Pulling on it, I tried getting the shit out of my throat because the shit was starting to hurt.

"Oh no, don't mess with that. You will tear everything inside of your throat. We put that there because we did not want you to talk at all. You were brought in with multiple gun shot wounds, including one to the side of your neck," she said to me. "Sir if you calm down, I can properly help you," she said. Giving up my efforts in getting the shit out, I allowed her to do things her way, as I relaxed and let her take over. Once she had successfully extracted the shit from my throat, my mouth felt sand paper dry, and very itchy.

"Water," I said as my voice came out high pitched like a bitch and barely above a whisper. Grabbing a pitcher from the stand by my bed, she filled a cup with water and tried to help me drink it. Pushing her hands away from me, I held the cup myself with shaking hands as I struggled to bring the cup to my lips for a drink. The water went everywhere but my mouth when I tilted it towards me.

"Fuck!" I barked, but my voice was so high pitched and lacking in base that it didn't have the effect behind it that I intended. Instead of laughing at me, the nurse simple took the cup from me, again filled it with water and instead of trying to assist me again, she instead handed it back to me. Looking at her for a second, I took the cup from her and tried it again. This time even though I got water everywhere, at least it went inside of my mouth as well. I drank from the cup like I had been walking in the desert for months with no water, that's how dehydrated a nigga was. Two cups of water and a bed full of soaked sheets later, and I finally felt like my thirst was quenched. Returning back to my original task of getting out of this bed, I swung my legs over the side of the bed. My adrenaline was racing, and I had murder on my mind. I didn't fully remember how I got to the hospital, but the fact I was supposedly shot was enough motivation for me to get my ass up and see what the fuck was going on. The last thought I had before I attempted to stand up was somebody was dying tonight. As soon as I stood up, I immediately hit the ground as my legs gave out on me and I went down crashing into machines along the way. Quickly running over to me, I complained the entire time as she helped me up and back into the bed.

"Don't fucking touch me," I spat, pushing her hands away from me.

"Calm down Mr. Carter," she said as a male nurse came into the room followed he another nurse. The noise had attracted quite an audience. But if these bitches wanted a show, a nigga was most definitely gon' give them one. I couldn't work my legs right now, but these hands were still official. Never taking my eyes off the big nigga with the extra small, green nurse's outfit on, I waited like a predator for him to come near me. I was gon' hit his big soft ass two times and told him quick as fuck. I was getting out of this bitch, by choice or by force. Some shit had popped off and I needed to get the fuck out of this bed.

"Calm down sir," dude said to me walking towards me with a needle in his hands. Soon as he got within arm's length, I hit his ass in the throat and as he fell towards me, I grabbed the needle and held it to his neck.

"Back up," I told him leaning on his weight for support as I attempted to pull myself up just as an older black nurse came into the room. It was something about her that caused me to pause and focus on her. She had a sense of familiarity about her.

"You don't want to do that, Landon. Drop that needle and get your behind back in that bed. You've busted your stitches carrying on like crazy, and you bound to get an infection. That's what you want? To have your legs amputated and never walk again?" She said in a stern but authoritative voice. Shit, a nigga don't know why my black ass listened to her, but pushing dude away from me, I did exactly what I was told and got my ass black in the bed."

Nigga, yo ass going soft as fuck in this hospital, you most definitely need to get the fuck out," I scolded myself.

"What's wrong with me?" I asked her, clearing my throat and laying back on the pillows breathing heavily like I'd just run a marathon.

"Dr. Morrison will be in shortly to explain everything to you. In the meantime try and relax. You have your entire family in the waiting room, worried sick about you. That wife of yours has refused to go home and even get cleaned up since you were brought in here and you carrying on like that. That beautiful baby of yours is out there as well. You really want your family to see you behaving like this, chile?" Hearing that my family was here alive and well, calmed me all the way down. That was my only concern at this point.

"Take me to them," I said.

"When you calm down, and after the doctor comes in to speak to you, I will personally make sure they come back here and see you," she said. "Now let me get you hooked back up to everything before you pass out. You need to come to terms with the fact that you were shot and your body is damaged. You need to properly heal Landon before you go carrying on acting crazy," she said propping my legs neck up on pillows, and hooking the IV back in. "Now I'll bring you some ice chips for your throat and some food in a bit. Don't you have them coming back and telling me you are clowning," she said as she fluffed my pillows up and walked out the room.

"Who was that nurse?" I asked the nurse who has remained in my room.

"That's Nurse Betty. She's the new head nurse here in our trauma unit." The name didn't ring a bell at all, yet she had this familiarity about her that I couldn't quite put my finger on. Just when I had managed to get comfortable, the door again opened, and this time a doctor walked in.

"Look doc, no offense, but I have my own private doctors, so if you would gone give a nigga them release papers, I'll get out y'all hair and be on my way. I'm sure they wil get a nigga right, but this hospital bed shit, naw I ain't with this shit," I said getting straight to the point. I felt exposed as hell right now. I didn't have a vest on, a gun, or any fucking thing. I didn't like feeling this vulnerable and helpless. Hell, each time the door opened, a nigga heart rate sped up, because it's nothing for a nigga to touch me right now. I know ain't no guards at my door, so a nigga was a damn open target. I might as well have a damn arrow outside my room saying "here I am."

"You were brought in here, having sustained multiple gunshot wounds. You were shot twice in your legs, and once in your neck. You are very blessed the bullet missed all major organs, but you are going to have to undergo intense physical therapy to walk again. The nerves in your leg were severely damaged. Although the wound to your neck isn't as bad as it could have been, we still have not removed the bullet. It's nowhere near any arteries, but it is lodged pretty deep inside of your neck. We have you on fluids to kind of push it up a bit, but surgery is a must to prevent it slipping any further down. You are in no shape to be released, so I'm sorry, but I cannot sign off on that at this time," he refused, pushing his glasses up nose some more.

"Nigga, you can't legally hold me in here. I know my rights, and all I have to do is sign a consent form releasing the hospital of all liabilities in the event a nigga dies. Now, I already done told your monkey ass that I have my own team of doctors, and I'll hire my own physical therapy team, if and only if I need to. I taught myself how to walk once before when I was a lil' nigga, and I can do the shit again. Now go get my wife and seed, and then those release papers. I got shit to do. And, I want you to start talking that you can't release me shit again and watch how fast my lawyer fly up here. I'll hit this hospital with so many lawsuits, your damn great grand kids will still be in debt. Shit you don't want to play big bank takes little bank with me doc, because I could bet money, I can buy five of these damn hospitals and won't even miss that chump change," I spat. I wasn't trying to sound cocky, but a nigga was merely stating facts. I was cranky, these cheap ass polyester sheets were irritating the fuck out of my skin, I was hungry as hell, still in a lot of pain, and just wanted to see my girls. This was not the damn time to try me. Getting the hint that I was not playing with his ass, he quickly grabbed his clip board and scurried out of my room like he had fire under his ass.

KNOCK! KNOCK!

I heard someone at the door, about five minutes later. Thinking it was Tommie, I got really excited as I sat up and ran my fingers through my waves. The smile I had quickly faded as two suit and tie niggas walked in. *Here we go with they ass,* I thought as they pulled out their badges. I already knew the routine, and how this was about to go.

"Good afternoon Mr. Cater, I'm detective," the big one started, until I cut him off.

"Look, I don't know nothing, and I didn't see nothing," I said.

"We are not the enemy here, we trying to help you."

"How?" I asked them, just to see what the hell they had to say.

"Isn't it obvious? We are trying to help catch whoever tried to kill you. You are lucky to be alive, but clearly you have a target on your back. A couple months ago, somebody shot up a local clothing store that you are part owner of, and now you was involved in a deadly shooting. Seems to us the common denominator in all these incidents is you," the black detective said.

"Naw, I was just in the wrong place at the wrong time," I said.

"Both times?" the black detective said with his eye brows raised.

"Yep, what are the odds?" I said.

"It would be in your best interest to accept our help. At this point you're either a suspect or victim," the white defective said.

"I'll have my lawyers contact you, and he'll decide which one I am. As a matter of fact, I'm feeling harassed, so I'ma need y'all to exit my room," I said.

"No problem, we'll be seeing you soon. By the way, what is your affiliation with Henry Snibbs?" They asked me. I burst out laughing because I knew their asses would eventually get to that being that it's an ongoing investigation. Smoothly I said,

"I have no affiliation with him." They stupid ass thought I was going to show any signs of nervousness or break out in a sweat, shit a nigga was built for this shit. Smirking at them as they walked out, I leaned back on the bed looking up at the ceiling. All I wanted was to get up out this hospital and get home to my girls. I needed to enjoy as much with them as I could because I planned on being in the streets night and day, until I found out who caught me slipping. I wasn't gon' let shit ride. Them niggas was gone have to feel me or kill me.

Love & Hennessy 4

CHAPTER 3
"MIRACLES HAPPEN EVERYDAY…"

TOMMIE

"I'm glad you are not this dramatic bae, because I definitely couldn't deal with that," I heard Dom say as my eyes fluttered open. Jasmine was standing over me with a cool towel as nurses rushed towards me with a gurney.

"I'm fine," I told them

"Shut the fuck up Dominic," Jasmine yelled at him as she helped me up off the floor.

"What? I'm saying though. That shit was hella dramatic," he said. "Noooo…," he mimicked me as he did a fake falling out. When he did that, my baby who was sitting up on Mariah's lap started to laugh.

"See uncle's baby even agrees with me," he said.

"Fuck you Dom," I said laughing as I walked over to a chair and sat down.

"Ma'am you just took a pretty nasty fall, you need to let us look at you," One of the nurses insisted.

"I'm fine, I need to find out what's going on with my fiancé," I said, brushing them off.

"Well before you fell and didn't even let the nigga talk, he was saying that Ghost ass is fine. Matter of fact, nigga back there talking shit and cutting up. I knew his ugly ass was okay , had y'all worried and shit. Ima fuck him up for that. Got my baby up here looking like raggedy Ann and hitting the ugly cry," he said, laughing. Hearing this, my heart filled with so much joy.

"Oh thank God," I said as happy tears begin to fall down my face. I wouldn't know what I would have done had he not been okay.

"Oh no you didn't. Nigga, you tried it. Yo ass was just over there crying and swinging your arms in the air like Trey off Boyz in the Hood," she said as she too begin mimicking him. I couldn't do nothing but laugh at their clown asses. They were made for each other because they both weren't wrapped too tight in the head.

"Whatever," he said not having a comeback for her.

"When can we go see him?" I asked as I got up and walked to Mariah and picked my baby up.

"Daddy is okay, Royalty." I said spinning her around in the air with a huge smile on my face.

"You might want to put them clothes on that your sister brought for you before you go back there. You looking like the chick off *The Ring* right now… like your ass just walked out somebody's TV, and about to get that nigga," Dom said. This time even Jasmine was laughing.

"I'm sorry baby sis, but he is right. You got your hair all over your head and dried up blood on your dress. You don't want your man seeing you like that." Looking down at my clothes, I mumbled.

"My baby loves me regardless."

"Yeah he does, but we both know Ghost would roast the fuck out of your ass," Dom said. Pausing to think it over, I reflected on my pregnancy when he didn't let my ass live with the jokes, so I knew Dom was right. Ghost was worst than Dom's ass when it came to flaming somebody up.

Without having to ask, Jasmine walked over to me and passed me the duffel bag she had packed for me, Royalty out of my hands. Offering her a smile, I happily accepted the bag and skipped off down the hallway to freshen up. I was going to see my man and couldn't be happier. It felt like years of separation, when it was merely a day.

***

"Landon it's not like it's permanent, but you need it baby," I said trying to reason with him to get into the wheelchair. I had convinced him to have the surgery here at the hospital, and then we would handle private care at home. He still had to undergo physical therapy to fully walk again, and here he was, pitching a fit about being in a wheelchair.

"Man fuck all that, the fuck a nigga look like rolling around in a damn wheelchair?"

"Okay well, how the hell do you think you gone get around then?" I asked him with my arms folded across my chest.

"Those doctors don't know what they talking about. Shit, I'ma real nigga. That pain ain't shit," he said as he held onto the table using it as a crutch to stand up. Once he was steady on his feet, he said,

"See told you," just as he went tumbling down to the ground. As if right on que, Nurse Betty walked through his open room door wheeling a wheelchair in.

"Right on time," I said to her.

"Still just as stubborn as ever," she said shaking her head at Ghost.

"Tell me about it," I said, laughing. Walking over with the chair she said,

"Now let's try this again, and this time get in this chair," she said as she helped him off the ground and into it. Surprisingly he got into the chair without so much as one complaint. Hell I need to know her damn secret. We been arguing about this damn wheelchair for literally an hour now.

"Now if you don't know of any good physical therapists, I'd be happy to recommend some to you," she said to him rolling him out of the room as I walked behind her with our bags. Every since the moment I found out he was alive and well, I hadn't left his side. I had a bed moved into his room, and been camped out here every since.

"I'm damn sure not having strangers in my house that I don't know. You got the job," he said to her as we got on the elevator.

"I appreciate the offer baby, but I'm a nurse. I'm not trained in that area. I can vouch for anybody I recommend to you."

"Naw. I don't want them, I want you."

"You also want to walk again, and I can't help you do that. Now if you need me to come over and check on you and make sure you taking the medicines you were prescribed, I can do that," she said. Feeling some type of way about her saying that because as his fiancé, that was my job. I said,

"Thanks Nurse Betty, but that won't be necessary, I can handle it-," I was saying until Landon cut me off.

"Bet. You can do that, a nigga definitely need you." He said as we got off the elevator. I cut my eyes at him as we rolled into the lobby where Jas, Dom and a few out their men were waiting. Still in the dark about who shot at us, Landon wasn't taking any chances on getting caught slipping again, so he had upped his security detail. I'm positive that wheelchair won't make him sit his ass down long enough to heal either before he's back in the streets to find the responsible party.

"Look at this faking ass nigga right here. Boy if you don't get your crippled ass out that chair and quit playing and shit," Dom said dapping Landon up with a big smile on his face. He can fake all day like he wasn't worried about him, but I know those tears, and the worry was real. The love they had for one another and bond was something rare to come by. I know it crushed him to even think something had happened to him.

"Fuck you, ole Jimmy Neutron, leave it to beaver looking ass boy," Landon shot back causing even Dom to crack up laughing. All I could do was shake my head at both their clown asses. This happened each time they were around one another.

"Here's my card with my phone numbers listed on them. Just give me a call and I'll stop by and check on you. " Nurse Betty said. handing Landon a card with her information on it.

"You not coming with us?" He asked and I prayed she said no. I liked her, but at this point, I was completely over her ass. I could barely take care of my man for her. At first I appreciated her assistance, but now I was glad to be leaving the hospital. Smiling, she said,

"No I'm on the clock and have other patients to tend to right now."

"Darn, I hate to hear that," I said sarcastically, as I got in the car after helping Landon's stubborn ass in. He so strong willed, it's gon' take a while for him to accept help and to understand that he can't beat this thing on his own. Saying our good byes, Dom and Jas got in their car to follow us home while half the men jumped in the car with us, and the other half jumped in black SUV's behind us. I was more than ready to get home to my baby, and start the process of putting this whole thing behind us, although I knew with a man like Ghost, that was easier said than done.

***

Walking into my living room after having just left the hospital with Jasmine visiting Vivian, who I could care less about, I put my keys on the table.

"Bae, you hungry?" I asked Landon who was currently in the living room with his legs propped up, watching TV. He has Royalty sitting up on his lap, and they both had their eyes glued to whatever show they were watching. They looked so adorable that I had to pull out my phone and snap a pic for the gram with the hashtag like father like daughter. I loved the unbreakable bond the two had formed in the short time that we've had Royalty, but I was also jealous because my baby preferred Ghost over me.

"No I fixed them something to eat already," Nurse Betty said walking downstairs carrying a pillow. Walking over to Landon, she lifted his legs, and rested the pillow on the table, placing his legs back down.

"What I tell you about keeping your legs elevated."

"They was on the table, that's elevated enough," he said, not even looking up from the TV. I just rolled my eyes. She was slowly working my nerves because everything I, the woman of the house, was supposed to be doing, she beat me to it. It's bad enough I had to compete with the team of nurses, and Mariah for a spot to take care of Landon and Royalty, now I had to deal with Betty. I know she meant well, and she's been wonderful with Landon, I just wanted to feel wanted by my man and child.

"You mind if I speak to you in the kitchen?" She asked me.

"Sure," I said walking behind her back into my kitchen. Reaching into her purse, she handed me a pill bottle. With my face all balled up, I just looked from the bottle to her.

"Calm down child, these are prenatal vitamins, I started you a prescription because I knew you hadn't gotten around to it. That's not good. How are those stitches feeling?" She asked me with a look of concern on her face. She made it hard to be mad at her when she did things like this. It's still something I didn't trust about her. Like, what was her motive for doing everything that she was doing for us? Money? What?

"Thank you," I said, accepting the pills.

"I know you haven't told Landon yet, so when do you plan on telling him?"

"I don't know, soon. I'm thinking of a creative way to tell him," I said.

"After what you guys just went through, life is too short for that, baby. Just tell him."

"No disrespect, but I've never had a man that was happy his woman was pregnant, so I want the news to be memorable for both of us. I won't wait long, just until after my first trimester is complete and I can know the sex. I don't care about a gender reveal party, I want that moment to be private, and his only to partake in. I have a feeling it's a boy, but I know if it's a girl, he will love her regardless," I said confidently.

"Okay baby, well I'm about to get out of your hair. It's time for my shift to start," she said as she grabbed her purse and keys off the kitchen table. I made a mental note to keep my eyes on her ass.

CHAPTER 4
"SHIT GETTING CRAZY IN THESE STREETS...."

DOM

Shit was getting crazier in this streets by the day, but a nigga was built for this shit. Hell, this was the shit I lived for. With Ghost out for a minute, it was my job to step up and handle shit accordingly. First I found out the nigga Kenneth was Jackie's baby daddy and ex pimp. The shit all made sense now. His bitch ass trashed my store and was on some fuck shit because I took his hoe from him. I used to love Jackie and still care about her, so I try not to disrespect her ass but damn, a nigga acted like she was a money maker or some shit. Like I took his bottom bitch. I know niggas ain't paying her ass no more than five dollars, shit if that! Maybe before the drugs she was seeing big money, but now that shit was dead game, so I wasn't fully understanding this niggas motive. But when he came for Jas, that's where he signed his death wish at. Since the nigga fucked up over 20,000 in merchandise at my store, I decided to return the favor by running down on his camp and fucking shit up. I was about to make his blocks so damn hot, that the only pussy he was gon' be selling when I got through with his ass, was pussy cats. I had called in a few favors, and got all the information off dude that I needed including where the nigga laid his head at, which wasn't even in New York, it was ATL. I planned on touching down real soon that way, so it wasn't nowhere that bitch could run to at this point. I was gon' fuck with him until it drove him crazy before I killed his ass. However, if I found out he had anything to do with Ghost catching heat, I was deading that bitch and his whole fucking family. Now that I think about it, the break in and shooting didn't happen that far apart.

"Yo, what up cuz '," Justice said as he got out of his car.

"Damn nigga took you all fucking day," I said to him as I dapped him up. Justice was a nineteen year old nigga on your squad. Unlike majority of our crew, he didn't stay in Jersey, he was a local. Although he was reckless as fuck and wild, he always came through to get the job done, and I actually trusted his lil' ass, something I couldn't say for everybody. Even though he was on our payroll, him and his lil' crew, the young wild niggas, did their own thing on the side. Them lil' niggas was slowly making a name for themselves from robbing, murder for hire, kidnapping, etc. You name it, them lil' niggas was doing it. I didn't knock their hustle though, long as they was always available when I needed them, knew, understood that I would pop one of their asses and their entire family, just to go home and fuck my bitch like ain't nun happened if they ever tried to fuck with me, and never played with me, it was all good with us.

"Shit you do realize a nigga can't grow wings and fucking fly to this bitch right?" He said , pulling a blunt out of his pocket firing it up. Lil' nigga had heart, I give him that, but his ass was also cocky. I see I was gone have to put him on his ass one day soon.

"Nigga with them big ass ears you could have fooled me ole dumbo looking ass," I said letting his ass have it.

"I know your ass ain't tryna crack, ole light skin ass Keith Sweat," he said.

"Boy you tried real hard with that one huh? Ole Oscar Mayer Weiner looking ass boy. Bitch you look like a bootleg Biggs off *Shottas*," I said letting his ass have it.

"You need to wash them dingy ass dreads," I said.

"Naw, I'ma stop you right there, all my bitches keep my shit together. You a damn lie. I bet I can take yo bitch," he said.

"Don't catch a bullet talking reckless," I shot back laughing. I wasn't tripping off his slick ass comment. If it were anyone else, we would have been in blows, but I fucked with the kid. Looking at his freshly twisted hair, I couldn't even argue with him on that shit anyway because them hoes was clean.

"Whatever nigga, now back to business. I need you and your crew to shut this block down. Any hoe you see on this block, it's a wrap for their asses. Ain't no pussy getting sold today, tomorrow, or the next day. Shit a wrap. Also, you see that hoe house right there," I said pointing down the street to the house I took Jackie from. "Run up in that shit, take what you want, and do what you the fuck you want with whoever you want."

"Shit what if niggas get out of pocket with us? You know my niggas don't really kidnap niggas no more. That shit dead."

"Naw niggas want smoke, dead they ass, just save this fuck nigga for me if he ever come around. You can rough him up a bit, but I don't want him dead. Ima play with this nigga until he beg to get killed," I said handing him a picture of the fuck nigga Kenneth. "I don't want all this done at once, start small. Hell, have some bitches jump a few of the hoes, shit like that. I want you to fuck with his money every day. If them hoes move to another block, have some bitches follow their asses. Save running in the house for last, or better yet, wait for my instructions," I said, cutting the conversation short and popping the locks on my car.

"Shit bet that up. But ima put some hoes on that for you. I got the perfect chicks in mind for the job," he said rubbing his hands together. Hopping inside my car, I said,

"Make sure it's not some hoes you fucking because them nappy headed hoes will forget they supposed to be fucking them bitches up, and start fucking each other up," I said laughing as I closed the door, pressed the start button, and took off down the road. A nigga had to go interview folks yet again at the shop. I would leave it up to Julius, but I've seen his friends, and I can only deal with one bitch at a time. Fuck around and catch a charge for popping one of them niggas for saying some slick gay shit to my ass. I already be having to get on Julius ass about that shit. I sometimes let him slide because his gay ass was kinda growing on me now. I found myself treating him like the bitch he looked like. Be waiting for the nigga to get in his car at night since it's dark, and hell last week, a nigga was getting out of pocket with him, and I almost beat dude's ass! If he didn't open his mouth, he did look like a full-fledged female, he just couldn't mask that deep ass voice, no matter how high pitched he tried to sound. But, I fuck with him the long way and at the end of the day, I really considered him family, and would pop a nigga quick for him. I was lowkey like an overprotective big brother in a sense. Hell I could make all the jokes and gay cracks in the world, but let you say something and it's up there.

***

"Next," I said for the hundredth time. It was late as fuck at this point, and a nigga was hungry as fuck, and tired. These hoes and niggas were working my last fucking nerves. The bitches thought they could suck some dick to get on, and hell a few of them were bad as fuck. If I wasn't rocking with my baby the long way, and she wasn't carrying my baby, I would have definitely let a few of their asses suck on this anaconda. Wouldn't have hired their asses though, this is my place of business, and I took it very serious. Hell the niggas were even worse, thinking Dom from around the way was gone look out. Shit I definitely wasn't fucking with it.

"You done passed up on everybody, hell I don't know if there is anybody else out there. You need to let me in control of this," Julius said, looking the guy I just dismissed up and down lustfully.

"Aye bruh, stop that gay shit on the clock."

"If you haven't noticed, I am sweeter than sugar, so I can't stop that gay shit," he said flipping his long ass weave over his shoulders.

"No shit Sherlock, but while you on the clock, you can't check out no niggas," I said.

"And you need to stop looking at fish then," he said.

"Shit that's different, I'ma man, that's what we do. I ain't tryna fuck none of them hoes though."

"I'm gay that's different, ima queen, I'm not tryna fuck none of them though," he said throwing my own words back at me. Before I could open my mouth to say again, he said,

"I'm tryna get fucked though."

"I'm done," I said picking up my phone and walking off, just as a bad ass chick walked in. I almost did an about face to do her interview she was just that fucking bad, but that nigga Julius was gone make me fuck him up if I stayed. I didn't expect her to stop me and say anything though, but she did.

"Hi Dominic, I'm Synthia, I'm here for an interview," she said sticking her hand out for me to shake.

"Nice to meet you Synthia, my manager Julius will be conducting your interview for you," I said shaking her hand, then high tailing it out of there fast as fuck before I got myself in trouble. Checking my custom made rolex day date watch, I saw that it wasn't that late, I planned on swinging by to see Ghost before I went home to my baby.

CHAPTER 5
THESE NIGGAS JUST WONT FUCKING DIE.......

KELINA

Getting word that Ghost and his bitch had survived the shooting after I know I put at least six slugs into that car really pissed me the fuck off. First, Dominic didn't die after I popped his ass in the back, and now Ghost ass was alive.

"These niggas got nine lives like they cats or some shit?" I yelled in frustration punching the table.

"I keep telling you that you tryna do a man's job and you not built for this shit," Kenneth said.

"And what's a man;s job? Because I recall you going to Fly Guy's and throwing clothes on the floor. Who the fuck did you pop though?" I asked him, rolling my eyes. I don't know why I even agreed to link back up with them. Well yes I do, because my money was drying up fast, and I needed the bread that Vanessa had promised us. I still wasn't ruling out popping both their asses and keeping the money for myself though.

"Bitch fuck you, you know what's up with me, these hollow tips will hit a nigga so quick, make their shoulders lean back. I wasn't tryna kill the fuck nigga when I fucked up his shop, the nigga wasn't even there, I just got under that nigga's skin. Unlike you, when I dead that fuck nigga, he gone stay dead, and know I did the shit. Meanwhile, you running round here shooting niggas in the back, kneecaps, and side, and still ain't making shit shake. Shit you can't aim right because your scary ass be too busy tryna get away," he shot back.

"Naw I don't know what's up with you, you fake ass wanna be pimp . Everything about you fake as fuck and suspect with them fake ass alligator shoes on, and fake ass mink coat. You hollering bout them hollow tips will hit a nigga quick and make his shoulder lean back, bitch you a shooter with no gun. Fuck the shoulders, I'm tryna make their fucking skull lean. Talking about some damn getting under his skin, fuck nigga getting under somebody skin and actually pulling the trigger are two different things so shut your stupid ass up," I shot back as I got up from the table. He had pissed me off just that fast, and I was sick of his shit.

"Enough," Vanessa said as she walked into the room. "Both of y'all sound stupid as fuck, and neither one of y'all have done shit."

"I killed Henry," I said, reminding them that's the shit that put all this into motion.

"That ship has sailed. You did, but what else have you done? Let's not forget I took out a key player in this game and left the game wild open to take over," she said, referring to her shooting her own twin sister Vivian.

"Newsflash, she's not dead, just like Ghost didn't die," I said bursting her bubble.

"Just like Ghost, she down for the count, and she's not dead YET. I have that covered though, she definitely isn't waking up any time soon. I've been playing the grieving sister and keeping up with her health status. While she's down for the count, it's free reign over Menace, just like shit should be fairly easy since Ghost is damn near a cripple," she said having a valid point.

"That nigga Dom, more than likely beefed up security for Ghost though," Kenneth said.

"Get off the nigga's dick," I said.

"If y'all don't work out this stupid ass arguing, y'all both will wind up dead. Dom can't be in two places at once , nor guard two people at once. If he guarding Ghost, that means nobody is guarding Tommie," Vanessa said.

"That's what security is for, and his men are some hard hitters," I said.

"Now, who's on the nigga's dick?" Kenneth said. "But V, I agree with you on that one, and her mother is in the hospital, so Kelina can snatch her old ass up out of there," Kenneth said.

"Nigga the fuck I look like Kim Possible or some shit? How the hell my ass supposed to kidnap her from a damn cancer facility? Fuck all that, I don't need to use anybody to get at Tommie's weak, ugly, fat ass. I can do that myself," I said.

"Now we both know that girl ain't ugly," Kenneth said as Vanessa shook her head in agreement. Fuck them that fat bitch didn't have shit on me.

"I like the idea of getting at her personally, I just don't think you can do the shit alone. Hell last person tried that shit is dead," Vanessa said referring to Tommie's baby daddy Rodney.

"Naw, I heard dude ain't even dead though," Kenneth said.

"Damn is everybody just surviving bullets and shit?" I said.

"Shit I don't know, I just heard they had a closed casket for his funeral. Some said he was in there, and some don't think the nigga dead. But, I know somebody who hates Tommie and Ghost just as much as you, and would help you take Tommie ass out," he said.

"Who?" I asked him.

"Amber," was his only reply.

***

I had been stalking the warehouse where I knew
Ghost used to hold meetings at for a few days. I even hacked
into all of his email accounts. Nothing, it's like he had
literally gotten Ghost. I had found him that night because
Tommie checked in at the restaurant, and even took a picture
with the hashtag date night with bae. I'd also been stalking
her social media accounts lately from several different fake
accounts that I had made, and I was still coming up empty
handed. I bet y'all wondering why the hell am I so obsessed
with Ghost all of a sudden, if we was just together. The truth
is, I've been bitter every since he made me get an abortion
with my baby, yet quick to play daddy of the year to
Tommie's ugly ass child. It's like my baby's life didn't
matter. We've been having sex on and off for years, yet he
never attempted to wife me up until almost a year ago.
Before then, Vanessa had already come to me with the plan
that she had, and I was all for it until me and Ghost got closer
as planned. Then, I had forgotten my reasoning behind
getting close to him. Shit that's all I ever wanted was for him
to see me for something other than a fuck buddy. Then,
Tommie's fat ass came back into the picture and ruined the
fairy tale that I had envisioned for us. So, if I couldn't have
my happily ever after, then that bitch wouldn't either. Both
of them was gon' feel the same hurt I felt.

Love & Hennessy 4

CHAPTER 6

CHELSEA

I didn't make any of these weak as books, so it's only right I debo my way into the final. I know y'all ugly asses been talking mad shit about me because of how shit when down with Tommie, Rodney, and Amber, but it's a reason why I never told Tommie that Karter was Rodney's son. See, I'm not sure when this hoe Tommie reinvented herself as this sweet angel, but this hoe is far from a fucking angel. I've hated this hoe for years, every since she told people that my daddy tried to rape her. He was sentenced to twelve years in prison, and ended up hanging himself halfway into his first year in jail. I know for a fact she doesn't know that Pon was my dad, but that didn't make me hate her any less. That's why I loved when fucked up shit happened to her, I've always gotten a good kick out of it. The shit made my day when the hoe would come around with her face caked up, tryna hide them black eyes, and trying to pretend that shit was all sweet with her and Rodney. Like she had the perfect man and perfect life. Hell I wasn't Amber's friend either because I stayed throwing hoes on Rodney knowing he and Amber were still fucking around. I didn't do it to fuck with Amber, I did it because I don't like that hoe Tommie. I never ever fucked Rodney though, but I thought about it a few times. But then I was like shit a bitch can't be catching diseases and shit with this nigga that's for everybody just to fuck with her. It wasn't that deep, I got satisfaction out of knowing he was out here dogging Tommie's ass. Pulling into Amber's house, I cut the engine and hopped out the car. She had been calling me all morning talking about come over to her house because it's urgent. I don't know what the hell it could be, but I was about to find out. Knocking on the door, I waited a few minutes until Karter opened it.

"What I tell you about opening my damn door? Come sit your ass down and wait on your grandma," I heard Amber yelling as I walked inside the house. Walking into her living room, I noticed some chick sitting on the couch.

"What's up," she said to me.

"Hey," I said waving to her. A few minutes later, Amber walked from the back with her boyfriend Kenneth.

"Damn bitch it took you long enough. I told you to be at my house early this morning," Amber said to me.

"Yeah and you didn't figure I had stuff to do? Stuff didn't just stop because you wanted me to come over. I'm here now," I said with a hint of attitude. She was already working my nerves. I know she noticed we didn't hang as much as we used to. With Tommie out the city, Amber no longer was an entertainment for me. The bitch was reckless, and involved in too much shit. She been hitting the drugs too damn hard if she thinks for one second that Ghost was just gon' let shit ride with her having them dudes to run up in that store like that. Shit she better use her baby daddy as an example of who not to fuck with. I had a bulletproof plan to get me, my girl, and our unborn child out the city and somewhere far away from this shit. A fresh start. Scanning everyone in the room, I just knew whatever she had to tell me wasn't good.

"So look, we've came up with a plan to come into a couple million dollars," Amber started which instantly got my attention.

"Like what?" I asked her.

"We snatch Ghost's baby, hold her for ransom, and once he makes the drop, we kill the little bitch and dip with the money," Amber said. This bout the dumbest bitch on the planet. I just know this hoe ain't say what I think she just said.

"Girl you called me over here for this dumb ass plan. Like we can get anywhere near Royalty without Ghost killing our asses," I said.

"I'll take care of Ghost," Kenneth said. I cut my eyes at him giving him the side eye. He could stunt for Amber all he wanted, but I knew a fake ass thug when I saw one. He most definitely wasn't built for that life he trying to live. Talking about some let him take care of Ghost. All these idiots was dying, shit I know who black ass wasn't going along with this dumb shit, and that's me.

"Well if y'all have it all planned out, what you need me for? Shit it's not like my ass can steal the baby. I openly shaded Tommie's ass every chance I got, she know I don't fuck with her. It's obvious at this point."

"Regardless, to pull this off, we need all the manpower we can get. Shit she knows none of us fuck with her, but that shit doesn't matter. We need to start casing out the place, and once we get Ghost out the way, we have to instantly attack. If we wait, Dom will put security on her," ol girl said, finally speaking up.

"That's Kelina," Amber said even though I didn't ask.

"I don't know," I said to Amber because although the shit sounded simple, I knew Ghost from around the way, and I damn sure didn't want them problems. Because A, I didn't have any faith in Kenneth's ass, and B I didn't trust ole chick sitting in the corner eyeballing me. Trying to see how I could use this situation to my advantage, I took a few seconds to think it over.

"Damn it's not rocket science. You either in or you not? At this point, you really don't have a choice, because we can't chance you running your mouth," Amber said pulling out a gun.

"Really, Amber?"

"Yes really bitch. You been suspect since the last time I told you some shit. Ain't nobody got time for that. Besides, don't act like your raggedy ass doesn't need the money, because your car is on its last leg, you stay with your momma, and let's be honest, that weave is tired. Now that we got that out the way, let's run over this shit again now that Chelsea here to make sure everybody know what part they playing in this," Amber said.

***

Putting my keys in the door, I walked inside and turned the lights on as I walked into the kitchen to grab a bottle of water before walking upstairs.

RING!RING!

Glancing down and noticing it was my girlfriend calling, I quickly answered.

"Hey baby," I said.

"Hey," she said barely above a whisper and sniffling.

"What's wrong?" I asked her becoming concerned.

"I'm probably going to have to find somewhere else to live because I don't have the rent money, and I have no idea where my child and I will go," she said her sniffles now having turned into a full out cry. My heart broke to hear her crying.

"Calm down baby, we'll figure something out."

"How Chelsea? I don't have the money, and even if I scrape it together for this month, I'll have three weeks to stress about getting it for next month. I can't keep living like this!" Briana said.

"Look baby, just hold on a little longer, I got something lined up that will take all of your problems away," I said to her.

"You promise?" She said.

"Would I ever lie to you? Trust me."

"What is it?" She asked me.

"Don't worry your pretty little head baby girl, let me worry about that," I said to her. After we got that squared away, we talked for another few minutes before she told me she would call me back. By this time, I was in headed towards the back of the house. I had just hung up the phone when I felt a gun on the back of my head. I threw my hands in the air in surrender and slowly turned around.

"Rodney? What the fuck dude?" I asked him as he stood there with one hand on his IV machine, and the other on a gun. Did I forget to mention he wasn't dead, and that I was secretly nursing him back to health.

CHAPTER 7
DID Y'ALL MISS A NIGGA......

RODNEY

Y'all knew a real nigga wasn't dead right? Like get the fuck out of here. Yall stupid like them hoes, if y'all let Carmen geek y'all ass up with that bullshit. Y'all actually believed I was out for the count? Shit real niggas don't die we just multiply. That was some sucker ass shit Ghost ass pulled, but shit I can't blame him, I got at him first, so I ain't tripping on how he came back. Nigga came back hard as fuck though. My beef wasn't even with my cousin, it was with that bitch Tommie. I jacked him for his shit because he was on some soft ass bullshit, nigga pussy whipped. I mean the pussy was good though I can't lie, but he wasn't supposed to let pussy come between us. I'ma miss that nigga when I pop his ass. Shit fuck y'all thought I was gone go out like a sucka? Shit I gotta get my lick back, fuck all the dumb shit. I gotta be more calculated with my attack this time, though. Gotta make sure my next move is my best move since he took damn near my whole crew of niggas out in that fire. I think a few survived, but they ass had gotten ghost because they was scared of Ghost, pussy ass niggas. I haven't heard from Monsta yet, but I told him about this place a long time ago, so If he was alive, and hiding out, he would eventually make his way here when he thought the coast was clear. Goes to show you your day one doesn't mean they A1. I ain't been rocking with Monsta long, but his ass more solid then Mikes bitch ass. I hope that bitch somewhere stankin'.

Know for a fact his rat ass would have folded under pressure. But, even a full clip couldn't put me down. I heard that boy caught some lead too recently. Sholl wish I could have been the one to do the shit. Lowering my gun, I rolled my IV machine back down the hall as I walked with it slowly. I was all fucked up. To be honest, I don't even know how I survived that night. I knew I was dead, nigga saw the light and everything. Chelsea found me on the ground damn near dead and somehow got me out here to my ducked off spot outside the city that nobody knew about. I can't even tell you what the fuck she was doing out there that night, but I was just glad she was there. Nobody, not even Kelly knew a nigga was still alive. Since Ghost set fire to the entire building, and Chelsea had a night gig at the morgue, I had her burn the body and drop it off at the hospital with my wallet Id, and etc in it. With the body burnt and my identification found, wasn't no need to try and get my dental records and shit. Let's be honest, it's not like a nigga was a law abiding citizen or some shit. They couldn't wait to get my black ass out their shit I bet. I can't lie though, a nigga had a playa made ass funeral. I had cancelled Kelly's ass before all this shit jumped off, but she was a real one. The bitch still made sure I had a fly ass funeral. I'm talking horse and carriage, the whole nine yards. Fuck her though, she was on some other shit, besides I only fucked with her in the beginning because her brother was moving some big weight. Shit, she promised me she would get me some bricks for the low and that shit never happened. Only thing ima miss, is my damn clothes. Fuck, a nigga used to be fly as fuck. The rest can be replaced. Day by day, I was slowly moved money into an off shore account. I move small amounts right now so shit won't raise red flags. I mean a nigga is dead and all, so shouldn't no activity be going on with my account. Especially since my name is the only one on all my shit. I wonder if Kelly went to the bank to try and withdraw some bread? I wish I could have been there to see the fucking look on her face when they told her she didn't have access to anything. Dumb bitch better try and live off the fifty racks I had stashed inside the house. And speaking of house, that's in my momma's name as well, so Kelly was really assed out. Walking into my room, I sat on the bed and got everything out that I needed to clean and change my bandages and remove this IV. I should have been off the fluids awhile ago, but shit since I popped the doctor, I was forced to stay on the shit longer than intended. When we got here, I had a doctor I kept on payroll come patch me up. Once I got to a point where I could move around on my own, I popped his old ass. I had become very paranoid and couldn't take any chances at this point. Shit I had Chelsea in the room each time he bandaged my wounds, or gave me any medicine, so she picked up on enough to help a nigga. The less people knew I was alive the better. I had a mind to kill her ass, but that would come a little later on, I still currently needed her. I knew it would be awhile before I was back up and running, and it was only a matter of time before Ghost and Dom came to ATL looking for whoever got at Ghost. I definitely still planned on killing his ass, I just knew how to pick and choose my battles, and this wasn't one I was winning solo, with no man power. As soon as I felt like I was well enough to fly, I was laying low in another state recuperating, regrouping, and building my army back up. Removing the IV from my arm, I unwrapped the bandages that went around my whole body. Green and yellow shit were coming out of my wounds. Nigga was getting a fucking infection because I didn't have all the proper medicine that I needed. Chelsea had a lil' bitch that she fucked with that worked at the hospital, and I kept telling her to get the bitch to get me some medicine. Hell, I would even pay the hoe, but she still ain't did the shit yet. I was too paranoid to be on these streets solo, or I would have been got the shit myself. I was regretting not bringing Kelly in, and killing Chelsea's ass the more the days passed. If she keeps this shit up, that's exactly what ima do. Hell Kelly would have gotten me a whole pharmacy by now. Shit even Tommie's fat ass would have tried to make something shake by now. After I was finished, on my way back to the kitchen, I overheard Chelsea on the phone with somebody talking about a plan they had to kidnap Royalty for ransom money. I wasn't upset until I heard the word kill. Now granted I didn't give a fuck about the baby in the past, but that still doesn't change the fact that that's my seed, so they had me fucked up. I couldn't do shit about it in the condition that I was in, other than kill Chelsea's ass. I couldn't pop whoever else was involved. Well not physically anyway, but if I wasn't good at shit else, I was good at fucking people up without even lifting a finger. I could especially manipulate the hell out of women, shit look at my track record. Id never tucked Chelsea, and still probably wouldn't give her this dick unless she let me hit her girl as well, but I'd definitely let her suck on this big dick. Shit give me five minutes with your grandma, and I bet I have her ass giving me her entire social security check, and tides for church. I was that nigga bandages and all. Shit I could hit the hoe with my IV in, that's how foolish I was. See I had almost went back on my word and let this hoe live, but talking about killing my seed had officially just signed her death certificate. A thought came to me as I walled inside the kitchen.

"Aye I think you should tell Ghost that Amber the one got at his shop," I said.

"Why would I do that? And it's not like he would listen to me," she said.

"Shit, cause I couldn't help but overhear you talking to Amber, and I know she a snake ass bitch. Shit, look how she did her best friend. That was her girl since free lunch. You think she won't snake you? All yo ass been talking about doing is getting some bread and getting away, seem like it's taking forever for that will to come back," I said because I had written up a will a few weeks ago making her my beneficiary so that I could give her 100 racks for helping me. Of course that shit wasn't happening, but she knew I was good for it, so she bit off whatever I told her. I did give her everything I had in my pocket when she'd brought me here, but then turned around and made her spend it all on me. I had her buy me clothes, sweat pants, boxers stuff like that, deodorant, and simple stuff like that. I couldn't risk her getting me anything that would cause some eyebrows to raise. She also bought all my favorite snacks.

"It really is taking awhile, and my girl needs that money. She about to get evicted, and stressed out. We need it," she said. Smiling on the inside because I was about to get my threesome and execute my plan at the same time. Shit was just falling in my lap.

"That's what I'm saying. Why split the money five or six ways when you can keep it all to yourself. Didn't you say your girl had a kid? Shit kids are expensive as fuck, take it from me. My ass got two. Plus bills start hitting, hell ten racks won't last but a month, and then what? I don't need a cut, that's all you, I just don't want to see you get played with you got a wife and child to think about," I said laying on extra thick with the wife card. I knew her sucker for love ass was hooked on chick. Lesbian or straight, I can mind fuck anybody.

"You right, the plane ticket a grip by itself alone, and then I want us to start over with new wardrobes and stuff," she said. *Gotcha*

"Right and shit you honestly think y'all would get away with that bullshit ass plan? You stand a better chance snitching on her ass for the money because I heard it's a bounty on whoever shot Fly Guys. And don't worry about how you gone contact them and remain anonymous so shit won't come back to you. Just made a fake profile with no picture and bogus name, that way it's no way they'll know it was you. You can have them wire the money to your girl account or some shit. Man if push comes to shove you think Amber won't be quick to try and throw you under the bus to cover her own ass? Hell I know this wasn't even your plan, " I said to her. I knew for a fact when Ghost went to kill that hoe Amber, she was saying Chelsea name. I hope they got who else was in on this plan as well. They had fucked up coming for my seed. Pausing for a second, she said,

"So I just have to write Tommie and say I want to collect the money?" On the inside I was bussing up laughing at this fucking idiot, but on the outside, I remained with a concerned expression on my face.

"Naw, see only those close to him would target Tommie, or only a female would write another female. Write Ghost... just say some shit like he can buy your services, and you'll solve his mystery like you Sherlock Holmes or some shit," I said.

"I'm down," she said, sealing her own fate.

Love & Hennessy 4

CHAPTER 8

I'M IN SOME DEEP SHIT.......

JASMINE

"I understand that you are a doctor as well, but this is not your field of study. Just please let us do our jobs," Dr. Bain told me again refusing to let me view my mother's charts, and offering me no other explanations other than the generic ones we tell patients. I wasn't new to this, I've been on the other side more times than I can count, so I knew he was intentionally railroading me. I wasn't having the shit, not when it involved my fucking mother! I would turn this entire wing upside fucking down. I was hot, hungry, fat, and was getting frustrated by the minute with him. I was planning on moving my mom home to undergo private care like Ghost was getting. The only reason my father had her in this facility was because she was receiving around the clock private care in a private area of the hospital by herself. However, she still had not woken up, and it stressed me out more and more as the days went on.

"Actually this is exactly my field," I said, back to him.

"Cardiac electrophysiologists deal with heart rhythm, heart monitoring, disorders, and things of that nature. You can hear from the machines that your mother's heart is extremely strong."

"That doesn't mean shit. Your fucking degree isn't any higher than mine, or makes you no more important than me. Me taking a look at her charts won't hurt you, since clearly all you have been doing is administering her fluids for the last two weeks. You have no fucking idea what's going on with my mother. So help me God if she fucking dies on your watch, they will never find your body, and that's not a fucking threat, that is a promise. For all we know it's a blood clot in her heart or something," I shouted at him. Pushing his glasses further up his nose, he cleared his throat before he spoke again.

"That's not why she isn't waking up, at this point her heart is the only strongly functioning part on her body. She's not breathing on her own, and hasn't since she was brought in. We also still have not detected brain activity. We believe the surgery caused her brain to shift to the back of her head somehow. We have experts coming in later this week to give us a second look. At this point, it's totally up to her whether she wakes up or not. You know how this works just as well as I do. And you also know that threatening the doctors does nothing for the patients in these cases, because it's out of our hands. We are not God. If it is his will for her to wake up, or stay sleep, we can only accept that," he said with sympathy in his eyes.

"Moving her to a hospital that specializes in neurology is also an option. But, at the point you need to be prepare yourself for the worst because unfortunately it's a 95 percent possibility," he said but I immediately interrupted him.

"Possibility that, what? Huh? What are you trying to say to me? Don't you even fucking speak that into existence. My mother is the strongest person I know. She will wake up, I know it. She is just tired that's all, she will wake up," I cried, looking over at my mom who looked like she was sleeping peacefully, I slowly walked back over to her bedside.

"You need to wake up you hear me? Your grandson needs you. Who else will I threaten to take my child away from if they don't change their attitude? You are mean, heartless, and hate my sister which I hate, but at the end of the day, you are my mom. We only get one mom in this world, and we definitely don't get do overs if something happens to her. I thought I was strong and could get through this, but I can't, mom. I can't live without you. I can't fucking breathe without you. Don't you dare do this to me. Don't you dare. Out of all the cruel things you've done in your life, you owe me this one, ma. I can't do this without you. I'm scared shitless to become a mother. You wasn't the best mother, but you raised me the best way you knew how. I went to medical school because of you. You stayed on me every minute of the day constantly blowing my phone up, and running off any guy I dated. I hated you for it, but with no guy around to distract me, I graduated with honors and top of my class. Mommy, I need you," I cried as I laid my head on her bed. I felt some arms wrap around me, and I didn't even have to look up to know it was my dad because I smelled his cologne. I had almost started to resent him because I never saw him up here with her, but feeling his hot tears on my neck let me know, and made me realize it just as hard for him to see her like this as me, if not harder for him. Even though he's cheated on my mom in the past, and had a child by her, my parents have been together off and on for almost 30 years. That's a lifetime and then some.

"Daddy, is mom going to be okay?" I asked him as I raised up and looked into his eyes. Growing up, my dad always made everything better to the point I thought he was super man. Instead of answering me, he instead leaned down and planted a kiss on my forehead.

***

KNOCK!KNOCK! KNOCK!

Hearing repeated knocking on my door, my eyes fluttered open as I lay there trying to fully wake up. As the knocking continued, I looked to my left at the clock which read 10:30 pm.

"Dominic's ass must forgot his key again," I grumbled as I sat up in bed. Since we've been back together, he's either at my house, or I'm at his, so we each have a key to the others place. Unlike me, he is forever forgetting his damn key somewhere, then will wake me up out my sleep knocking on the door and shit. Throwing my feet over the side of the bed, I slid them into my furry bunny house slippers, and stood up headed out of my room, down the hallways towards the front.

"He act like he couldn't have rung the doorbell or at least sent me a text letting me know to open the door he pulling up. Rude ass light skin nigga," I grumbled as I threw all the locks off the door and swung it open.

"Damn I wish you stop losing your key," I said as my voice trailed off. Instead of seeing my handsome but annoying ass boyfriend, I was staring into the face of my on again off again fling, Mark.

"Mark? What are you doing at my house at this time of night?" I asked him, looking past him at the car the men who guarded me sat in. I didn't want to give them any reason at all to call Dominic.

"Is that anyway to talk to the father of your child Jasmine?" He asked me walking closer, reaching out and rubbing my stomach. My eyes grew big as saucers when he did that.

"This is not your baby, this baby belongs to Dom," I said. He knew about Dominic just like Dominic knew about him. Smirking, he brushed past me without an invite into my home, he walked over to my wet bar, and helped himself to a drink. Closing the door, I walked into the living room with my hands on my hips I said,

"It's not your child, Mark. This is Dominic's baby."

"Jasmine just because you are in denial, and want to tell yourself that isn't my baby just to be with your thug boyfriend, won't make it true. I saw you post on Facebook that you are five in a half months pregnant, which would make you six months pregnant next week. This time six months ago, you were in my pent house suite in Atlanta bent over, taking these dick in any hole I chose to stick it in. Maybe your memory is a little fuzzy, and you don't remember certain details, but I can tell you fact wise that I nutted in that pretty pussy that entire weekend you were at my place," he said to me. I had honestly forgotten all about that week, it was right before I was scheduled to come home after having been working at the hospital in Atlanta, and Mark was there, and we've been on and off relationship wise for years, and continued hooking up regardless if we were together or not. I don't remember the dates exactly, it could have been a week or two before I came home to New York, or it could have happened like he said. I just know after I got home, I slept with Dominic one night when I caught a flat tire and he fixed it for me, and that was six months ago. He was the only person I was sleeping with after that as well. I couldn't be sure if the dates matched up with me having sex with Mark or not, because honestly that week of sex wasn't even memorable. I think I forgot it as soon as it was over. Realizing that there was a possibility that Mark could be the father of my child and that I didn't know for a fact who the father of my child was, caused me to become sick to my stomach as I pushed past him down the hallway into my room barley making it inside the bathroom before everything I had eaten that night came up. After I had heaved everything up in my stomach, I sat on my floor trying to steady my beating heart. *What the fuck,* I thought as I tried to gather myself together. After about five minutes, I found the strength to get up, brush my teeth and wash my face. The entire time I was throwing up,Mark didn't even have the decency to come check on me and make sure it was okay. Hell, he was so convinced that I was carrying his seed, yet his ass didn't even budge when I rushed to the bathroom. Every time I got sick, Dom was right beside me holding my hair back as I threw up or wiping me up after wards and helping to me brush my teeth and get myself together. It's like the baby brought out a completely different side of him completely different from anything he's previously shown. He's so excited about the baby, and the thought of having to tell him that it could possibly not be his made boring tears come to my eyes. I didn't want to lose him behind this and prayed that he was understanding in this situation. Walking back into the living room, this asshole had made himself comfortable on my couch like he didn't have a care in the world. I don't know what attracted me to his ass to begin with. Besides both being doctors, we have absolutely nothing in common, and he wasn't even somebody I'd associate with on the regular. My ass was just young and dumb, and really didn't know any better. Going into the kitchen, I grabbed a bottle of water, and some saltine crackers to eat because they helped me not to vomit everywhere. Eating a few in the kitchen, I walked back inside the living room with my eyes closed massaging my temples thinking of ways to explain this to Dom. I had a mind to do a pre paternity test right now, and keep it a secret from him.

"So what are you even doing at my house Mark?" I asked him still massaging my temples because I felt a headache coming on.

"Funny you should ask that bae, because that's exactly what I was about to ask this nigga before I popped his ass," I heard Dom say as my eyes immediately shot open. *Shit*

"Hey baby," I said as my voice trembled a bit.

"See I'm just in time for the party," Dom said.

"It's actually no party at all," Mark said. *This nigga right here just wants to die, the fuck.*

"Oh it surely looks like a party to me Dr.," Dom said. He was surprisingly very calm right now, which I wasn't sure if it was a good thing, or not. With a person like him however, I'd say it wasn't.

"So what I miss? Catch me up." Dom said. Trying to choose my words wisely, I said,

"Mark stopped by unexpectedly, but he was just leaving. Isn't that right Mark?" I said looking at him hoping he got the hint. I be damned if this smart but stupid ass idiot, opened his big ass mouth and said,

"No. I'm not leaving until we get some things worked out. And I'm here because she is carrying my seed." You could hear a pin drop how silent the room got. Like no lie I think an alien came down and used some type of freezing spell on us. I didn't hear any crickets outside, or anything. Nothing but dead silence until Dominic burst out laughing. *Lord Jesus please let me make it into heaven, because I know I'm dying tonight. Please watch out my mom, my sister and my niece.*, I silently prayed in my head. Closing my eyes, I waited patiently for the piercing feel of hot lead being pumped inside of me. When it didn't come, I opened my eye and survived the room. Dom had stopped laughing and was looking at Mark, who didn't look away. Like did I underestimate the kid? Was he like a thug who went to college or some shit? Dude was dead ass having a stare down with the devil, who happened to have a gun.

"Yo you dead ass funny. But no seriously it's time to go," Dom said.

"I didn't major in comedy, I majored in medicine, so if I'm being funny, I wasn't trying to be. But, my reasoning for being here hasn't changed. That's my seed that she-," was all he got out before Dom smacked him across the face with his gun. Breathing heavily up and down looking like fucking Satan himself, he said

"I don't give a fuck about what you talking about. All I fucking know is by the time I walk back in this fucking living room, yo ass better be gone," Dom said leaning down and grabbing him by his collar. "Cause bitch, if you still fucking here when I walk back in here, you leaving this bitch in a fucking sheet wrapped around you, or whatever the fuck my clean up crew chooses to wrap your fucking body in. Play with it if you want to, but you better ask Jasmine how the fuck a nigga get down. Bitch you'll find your square ass on the back of a milk carton playing these fucking hoe games," Dom said letting him go and he brushed past me headed to the back bumping into me unapologetically as he made his way to the back.

"Babe," I said to his back, but he didn't bother to turn around. Turning back to look at Mark, I didn't even get a chance to open my mouth before he bolted out the door like he had fire under his ass. He didn't even bother to close my door. Walking over to the door, I closed and locked it. Taking a deep breath, I counted backwards from ten before I headed to the back to have this showdown that I knew was coming. Instead, however, Dom met me halfway to the back and walked back past me and out the door. A couple hours later, I finally realized he wasn't coming back. Crying until I felt my eyelids get heavy, the last thought I had before I let sleep consume me was that I hoped this didn't destroy my family.

CHAPTER 9

NIGGAS BETTER KNOW ILL COME UP OUT THIS CHAIR IN A HEARTBEAT IF THEY GET OUT OF POCKET....

GHOST

"Lift up on five, okay?" my physical therapist said to me. She was this bad ass chocolate broad that Nurse Betty had recommended to me. I didn't know chicks like this would even be in this field, but it was no denying that she was a beast at what she did. When she got to five, I stood up from chair that I hated being in, and took one step forward with her help.

"That's it, put pressure on that leg," she said holding my arms as I took another shaky step forward. By my third step, she had released my hands, and I was managing to walk across the entire room solo. What should have taken just a few seconds to do, took me well into thirty minutes to do. I stopped a bunch of times, and fell down a few times, but I was determined to get back to the old me. It was killing me not to be out in the streets with Dom wrecking havoc, and trying to find out who shot me. I also needed to go check on my stores because I know that fool wasn't properly overseeing shit like I had asked him. If I had to practice all day until I got this shit together, I was gone walk again. I was coming back with a vengeance.

"Let's take a break," Tamara said, coming over to me after I fell again on my way back across the floor. I'm glad the floor had carpet, or I would be fucked up.

"Naw, I got it. Let me catch my breath, I'ma be ready to go again," I said laying back on the floor breathing heavily.

"Landon," she started but I cut her off. She was fine and all but only bitch got to call my Landon was my own bitch.

"It's Ghost to you," I said. Even though we've grown closer over the weeks, we wasn't that damn close.

"Ghost," she said with a hint of attitude. "You have to give your body time to heal. You can hurt yourself if you push too hard. You'll walk again, just trust your legs. Progress takes time, it won't happen over night."

"Shit a fucking lie, a nigga got shit to do, I'm walking up out this bitch tonight," I said. Fuck she thought this was. I was done with this whole cripple shit. Niggas prolly started thinking shit was sweet since I been down, but watch how I cut the fuck up soon as my feet hit the fucking ground. As I stood up, she reached out to help me up, but some how missed my arm complete and landed her hand instead on my dick. I was currently wearing grey sweat pants and a muscle shirt, and I noticed her ass had been eye fucking a nigga all afternoon. Y'all females kill me. You get mad at a nigga for staring at your ass and shit but will opening eye rape a nigga if he put on some damn sweat pants. Being that Tommie's ass been keeping the pussy away from me because she said she didn't want me to hurt myself, a nigga was rock hard just off of a damn touch. Even though she was bad as hell, I didn't want her, nor did I get hard for her.

"Well now," she said licking her lips while never taking her eyes away from my dick. Bitch act like she was star struck. Smirking, I said,

"This Tommie's dick lil momma, so let's just finish this session because my girl will most definitely beat yo ass if she catch you doing all this extra shit." I said. Leaning closer to me, she said,

"I'm no where near scared papi and with a dick like that, a bitch will most definitely take that ass whooping," she said, before she walked away to get my chair.

"You'll get an ass whooping and no dick lil' momma. Shit here I was thinking your ass had alopecia or some shit because your hair thin in certain areas, and this whole time it's because you was fucking with a nigga that didn't belong to you. Shit baby girl your ass better learn how to bob and weave at least, if you gon' put yourself in that situation. And I don't want that fucking chair anymore," I said pushing it away as I turned and walked slowly towards the door where I had some crutches at. The first tool to walking again, was to practice walking everyday where. Shit hurt like a bitch, but that wheelchair wasn't doing shit but enabling me, so I didn't need it anymore. Fuck that progress was a process bullshit, nigga wasn't tryna hear all that. Down boy, I commanded my dick as Tamara brushed past me and my eyes caught the sway of her hips Yeah, I most definitely was getting some pussy from my girl as soon as I made it through the door. My shit was about to jump through damn pants I was so hard, and shit it had nothing to do with Tamara's fine ass, and everything to do with weeks of being backed up.

***

"I don't like that hoe Tamara, I'm telling you she wants to fuck you. But, let me find out, and I'm beating both of y'all asses. You need to fire that hoe like tonight," Tommie said. She had been going on and on in a rant about Tamara since she got home. Completely ignoring her ass, I sent a group text out to my crew checking on my money, and sent a text out to my store managers seeing how things were going. I really needed to go to Landon's, my clothing store for men and women. It was as located in Harlem on 125th , but it was a very profitable store. I didn't have a manager right now because mines because that location didn't have a manager, and I usually worked there a couples times out the week. That was the location I was going to train Tommie for, but then this shit happened.

"Ghost, are you even listening to me?" She pouted.

"So I'm Ghost now?" I asked her with my eyes raised. Her spoiled ass only called me that when she didn't get her way. She wanted me to fire Tamara and honestly yes the hoe did want to fuck a nigga, but she was also damn good at what she did. So, I wasn't firing her. Unlike the fuck nigga she was used to, I knew how to keep my dick in my pants. A bitch can't be a threat to you if your nigga doesn't allow her to be, and that's something Tommie still hasn't gotten through her head. She is the only one who can trick her out of her place in my life, not these hoes out her, her. She gets in her own way. If you don't see your nigga doing anything, and he never gave you a reason to doubt him, stop fucking holding him accountable for what the next nigga did to you. Noticing Royalty had fallen asleep on my chest, I passed her back to her mother. My baby was getting bigger and bigger. After she took Royalty and walked out the room to go lay her down, I started operation get Ghost some of that lil' pwussy in my plies voice. Tommie's crazy ass had given me a bell to ring to signal that I needed her. The fact she was treating me like a weak ass nigga was really pissing me off on the cool because a lot of stuff she insists on doing for me, I was more than capable of doing myself. Since she insisted I used this gay ass bell, I was about to drive her ass crazy ringing this bitch, then fuck her ass to sleep. That's the only reason she was going crazy, she missed this dick just as much as I missed giving it to her. Her crazy ass only gave me this bell because she didn't want my staff of nurses in my face, so she called herself trying to do their job for them. Yeah I know I said I didn't like strangers inside my shit, but I paid a hefty price for private medical care in the event that I ever needed it. I vetted this staff myself, so I knew everything about them down to the last time they took a shit. I was a thorough nigga, through and through, but that didn't mean I still didn't want Nurse Betty here looking out for me. It was something about her that I couldn't put my finger on, and until I figured it out, I would keep an eye on her.

DING! DING! DING!

"Tommie," I shouted as I repeatedly rung the bell until she came running.

"What's up? What's wrong bae? She asked all out of breath. Trying to contain my laugh, I said,

"Yeah I'm cold, and I can't reach my water," I said reaching my hand out towards the dresser and pretending it was too far away. She looked wore out and tired as hell, but this was a lesson for her ass. Let these folks do the job they are paid to do. Shit only thing I need her to take care of was my daughter and this dick, and since Royalty was well taken care of, Tommie needed to be sucking and fucking her man.

"Okay I'll get you a blanket, and here is your glass, " she said, handing me the glass of water on the table.

"I don't want any of that room temperature water, get me some fresh water bae," I said to her. Rolling her eyes, she went downstairs to get me some fresh water. As soon as she left, I burst out laughing. My baby was funny as hell bruh. Hearing her stomping back up the stairs, I went back into sick mode clutching the sheets like I was really in pain.

"Here," she said handing me the water. Taking a sip, I said,

"Bae why you got me some cold water? This too cold for my throat," I said. Looking like she wanted to cry, she took the glass from me and was about to walk away from me until I grabbed her arm and stopped her.

"Fuck the water, your man need some lovin'," I said.

"No bae, we can't have sex because you're still not well," she said removing her arm from my grip and preparing to walk away until I hit her with a bomb.

"Today while I was working out with Tamara my shit rocked up so hard, I just knew I was about to burst through them fucking sweat pants," I said knowing that would get her attention. "You think she'll let a nigga break her in properly? I don't know, I think she can't take dick too well," I said.

"That hoe beat on sight," she said balling her fist up and she started back walking.

"Well before you beat the hoe, send her up here," I said again, pausing her instantly. Turning around, she looked at me wide eyed.

"Landon you would really say that shit to me. I would have expected that from Rodney but never you," she said.

"And I would expect my woman who I love to fuck me, but we see that ain't happening. And don't you ever in your fucking life speak that fuck niggas name in my house or presence. We know what happened the last time we got into it about him. Don't compare me to that mufucka. You know damn well I wouldn't touch Tamara with another nigga's dick, it's sad as fuck that I got to mention another bitch just to get your attention. You so hell bent on nobody being in my face, that you fucking neglecting your duties as my woman."

"Oh so not fucking you, is neglecting my duties."

"Hell yeah! But this not even fucking all about sex. Shit you don't even fucking sleep in the bed with me, what you scared you gon' hurt my legs? Nigga can't cuddle with his woman, suck the soul out his woman, or none of that shit. You are my woman, my wife, all I fucking need you to do is play that role. I have nurse and maids so fuck this stupid ass bell," I said chunking it to the ground. " I don't need you to self diagnose my situation, and tell yourself what I can and can't do treating me like a weak ass nigga when you know, that's not in my DNA. I need you to not only take care of Royalty, but your man as well that's ass I'm saying, but your ass to stubborn to even hear a nigga," I said. Reaching over to my table by the bed, I opened the third drawer and grabbed some lotion. "Guess I'll catch your slack."

Walking over to the door, she closed and locked it, then walked over to me. On the outside I was cool and collected, but on the inside I was like hell fucking yeah bae you better come get this dick. Taking the lotion out of my hands, she placed it back on the dresser.

"I'm sorry," she said to me before she moved the covers to the side, stuck her hand inside of my boxers, and pulled out my dick. She didn't ask no questions, or even play with it a bit before she spit on it, and went to work. The first contact of my dick with her wet mouth pushed a nigga straight to heaven. It's been so long since I felt that feeling that a nigga almost embarrassed himself and bust instantly. The most the sucked, the more my toes curled. Hell, my shit was throwing up gang signs and shit, the head was that damn good.

"Shit girl," I said grabbing a hand full of her hair guiding her head up and down on my dick. When she started jacking and sucking my dick at the same time, I lost it and burst all my kids down her throat. Looking up at me, she stuck her tongue out to show me my kids before she swallowed everything down her throat. That shit had me bricking back up instantly. This what I missed, my freaky ass woman. Not a damn caregiver.

"You know you done fucked up by letting me get that first nut out the way right? You better assume the fucking position and take all this dick," I said to her raising up. Without having to tell her ass twice, she quickly hoped up, stripped naked, and quickly got on all fours on the bed putting a perfect arch in her back. Before I blessed her with the dick, I spread her cheeks open and stuck my entire face in that pretty pussy.

"Fuck," she moaned throwing her head black in ecstasy. The reason I liked the fact that she got nasty with me, was because I was a nasty ass nigga. After sucking the soul out the pussy, I stuck my tongue in her ass and went to work. Gates ain't the only one who will eat ass, shit I eats it all. Without warning, I stopped my assault, lifted up, and plunged deep inside of her. Biting down hard on my tongue trying to contain the moan that almost escaped my lips, I tried to focus on anything but nutting as I stroked her deep and fast. This shit felt so fucking good, wet and tight. The way her walls was gripping my dick should have been a fucking crime. It was something different about the pussy, it felt wetter than usual, and shit was squeezing the fuck out my dick, she was so tight. I wasn't complaining by a long shot though. Feeling her knees buckling on her as she fell to the bed, I fell right behind her still giving her nothing but long strokes.

"Where you going, girl? Naw, don't fucking run now. You wanted to keep this pussy from daddy, shit now you gotta take all of it," I said, plunging even deeper inside of her. Putting her legs together, I got into a push up position, and started doing pushups in that pussy, really showing my ass. Putting her hand on my thigh trying to push me back, I slapped her hand away.

"Move your fucking hand and take this dick. It must not be yours. I guess you gone let Tamara work this dick for you then?" I said to her knowing that would piss her off, but make her go harder. Without warning, her ass turned over onto her stomach, and pushed me off of her causing me to fall backwards onto the end. Thank God I had a big ass California king, or my ass would have hit the floor. Coming down on top of me, she planted both her feet on either side of me, then came down onto my dick sitting down until all inches were inside of her. Then she rose up until just the tip was in, then slide back down slowly until I filled her up completely. She repeated this a few more times going slowly up, and sliding slowly back down. The shit was fucking my head up. When she rose up again, I quickly slammed her back down by her hips, and started working her from the bottom as a fast past.

"Fuck me back," I said moaning like a bitch not being able to hold it in any longer. Meeting me stroke for stroke, we went at it for the next few hours until we finally tapped out.

"Don't ever keep my shit from me again," I said to her, barely being able to keep my eyes open at this point. A nigga was wore out, and everything hurt from my back, to my legs, thighs, hips, shit it all burned. Fucking her long and strong took a lot out of me, but it was most definitely worth it. The last thought I had before I closed my eyes was that I hoped as many times as I busted inside of her, one of my little swimmers made it to her eggs because I needed me a jr.

***

"The guard at the gate wants to speak to you?" Mariah said walking into the room holding the phone we used to community with security. Taking it from her, I said, "Hello?"

"Ghost, it's a woman here says that she is your aunt," Marko said. I had given my Aunt Carol, Rodney's mom an open invitation to visit, but she wouldn't come unannounced, so I didn't know who it was. Pressing a button on the remote I was holding in my hand, a security monitor flipped down, and sure enough, I saw my auntie standing at the gate with bags in her hands.

"She good, let her through. Get somebody to drive her up the driveway," I said because I didn't want her walking about a mile to the door with all those bags. A few minted later, there was a knock on the door. Going to open it, I said,

"Auntie, what are you doing here? I asked her. I hadn't spoken to her since Rodney's funeral. Yeah I went to pay my respects, even though I was the nigga that put him there. He crossed lines that there was ultimately no coming back from. I hate that I had to end that way because that was more like my brother than my cousin, but if I could do it all over again, I'd still kill that nigga. He tried me on so many levels so many times, but playing me like a pussy ass nigga was the last fucking straw. Nigga stole a millions in cash and half a million in product and thought I was just gone let that shit slide? Like I wasn't gone see about that shit? No matter what I'm dying behind my respect. That man disrespected me in the worst way, and had to pay with his life. I would make sure his son was straight though. Tommie's ass has been bugging me for days to see what was going on with Karter. Even though his bad ass tried to call himself jumping me, and he didn't like me because I had to two piece and a biscuit his mother, I would still look out for the the lil' nigga. He had a fucked up father, and an even fucked up mother. Only solid person in his life was my aunt, and she was old, so no telling how much longer she had to make it.

"I can't come visit my favorite nephew?" She said walking inside the door. Grabbing her bags, I brought them in, and placed them on the couch.

"You can, but you usually call to let me know you are coming first. Is everything okay?" I asked her. Before she could open her mouth, Nurse Betty walked into the living room with me medicine and a glass of orange juice.

"I know you haven't taken these for the day," she said handing me the nastiest pills on earth.

"They nasty, and make me sleepy," I said. "Aunt Carol, this is the best nurse I've ever had, Betty." I said at the same time as my aunt hauled off and slapped her.

"That's not damn nurse, that's your mother," my aunt said as I stood there in shock.

CHAPTER 10

I'M ABOUT TO CATCH A CASE WITH THESE HOES…..

TOMMIE

Waking up from out of some much needed, I heard Landon screaming and yelling downstairs. Our house was huge, so to hear me screaming, something had to be going on. Becoming alarmed, I jumped up out of the bed and ran to the closet where I knew Landon kept his guns at. As the screaming grew louder, and a few more voices joined in, my fingers shook as I entered the code on the keypad. So many thoughts were rushing through my mind right now. *Lord I hope whoever shot Landon hasn't come back to finish the job*, I prayed as the safe swung open revealing stacks and stacks of money. Reaching past it, I grabbed his desert eagle, and glock nine. Making sure both were loaded, I ran out of the room and had both guns pointed out in front of me prepared to shoot first later and worry about the rest once I got to my man. Once I got down to the landing and came into the living room area, I saw Landon struggling to hold Rodney's mom back as she tried attacking Nurse Betty. Confused, I still didn't put the gun down as I walked further into the room. Mariah spotted me first, and let out a loud piercing scream causing everyone to temporarily direct their attention towards me.

"Why the hell you got those guns?" Landon asked me.

"I heard you screaming, I didn't know what was going on," I said with my hands still shaking. Even though I saw he was ok, I was still shook up as images on him slumped over the steering wheel of our car flashed into my head again. That's something I would never forget. This baby had me very emotional as tears begin falling down my face rapidly. Letting his aunt go, Landon ran to me as fast as his injury would allow him to, and just hugged me tightly. He already knew how I was feeling.

"It's okay baby, I'm okay…" he said kissing me on my forehead and rubbing my back. I just nodded my head. After a few minutes, we broke apart, and he took both guns from me.

"Remind me to change the lock on the safe because your ass getting too comfortable holding a gun, fuck around and shoot a nigga in his sleep," Ghost said laughing.

"Yeah you know I'm about that life," I said.

"What life? Girl you softer than a pillow, but it's okay bae, I'm not marrying you for that," he said. Cutting his eye at Betty and Carol, his face changed like lighting from happy to pissed off.

"What's going on?" I asked looking from them to him.

"Mariah, can you go check on Royalty please?" I said, turning my attention to Mariah, because I definitely wasn't missing this Jerry Springer show down.

"That's what the fuck I'm trying to figure out. Aunt Carol just dropped a bomb on a nigga, and told me Betty is my mother. Then, their asses started going at it like a nigga didn't just get some life changing news," he yelled.

"Ask this bitch," Carol said pointing to Betty.

"Oh no, I'ma come back to her. I'm on you now because a nigga grew up with you. Me and my ma dukes used to always come over your house before she died. So if that wasn't my mother, then who was it? And why you never told me the truth? Never Aunt Carol, why?" He said and I could tell this was very emotional for him.

"I just never knew the rights words to say, and it never was the right time," she said.

"Bullshit," Landon said yelling. He never yelled or cursed at her, so she knew he was pissed. "What about all the times I woke up crying for a mother I thought died? All the times I talked about my ma dukes? Them didn't seem like the right time to say oh your mother isn't dead, her ass somewhere probably being a hoe popping pussy for niggas, and didn't want you. A nigga could have accepted that shit, but no, you choose to lie to me knowing how I feel about that," he said.

"Now wait one fucking minute, I know you are mad, but what I won't allow you to do, is insult my character. I'm still your fucking mother," Betty said speaking up.

"You gave birth to me, but that doesn't make you my mother lady," Landon said coldly. Even I was starting to feel bad for both of them at this point. I mean I didn't like Nurse Betty but not because I thought she was a bad person, but because she was talking my mother and wifely duties away from me. But, because she took damn good care of my family, I was curious to hear what she had to say.

"Babe, just hear them out. Don't you want to answers? You'll never get them this way," I said squeezing his hand and I gave him a kiss on the cheek. Feeling his features softening up, I knew he was thinking it over. When he didn't respond, I said,

"I suggest you guys talk because I doubt you get another chance to do so," I said to them.

"I didn't want to give my baby up, my oldest sister, that raised Landon, and Carol bullied me into giving my child up, tricked me on drugs, and sent me away," Betty said. "Even in my drug induced state, I still mourned my child everyday."

"Liar, you abandoned him," Carol shouted.

"You've told that damn story to yourself so many times that you've started believing your own fucking lie. But, both of you made me give him to you. I didn't want to," Betty said.

"Why did they make you?" I asked her. Putting her head down, she said, because his father was one of the biggest drug Lords in the area, and we were in love. He was so happy when he found out I was pregnant, and even happier when he found out it was a boy. We were going to get married and start a family. But Justine, my own sister, was in love with my man. Carol never liked me because my father was the man our mother married and didn't get back with her father, so my own flesh and blood stole my child, tricked me on drugs, and ran me out of town. By the time I realized they had been feeding me drugs, I was too far gone, and a full blow drug addict," Betty said as tears ran down her face recounting a terrible time in her life. I even found myself shedding a tear.

"She raised my son as her own, and they allowed her to. My mother, and my sisters allowed that evil vindictive bitch to raise my child," Betty said.

"That's not how the story went," Carol said, finally speaking up.

"Well which part is a fucking lie?" Landon said. When she didn't respond, I know that crushed his soul. Hell, I never knew Ms. Carol would be capable of something like that.

"Wait but Landon's dad has always known about him, he just couldn't find him and when he finally did the cancer found him first. He didn't think it was odd Jackie was raising his seed?" I asked the million dollar question.

"When I had my baby, Santiago had just got knocked for a ten year bid that later got reduced to five years. The real kicker is that they had been stealing his drugs to pump me full of. Carol was fucking with Rodney's dad who would steal them for them. They told me if I didn't leave and stay gone they'd tell Santiago I had been stealing from him to get high. Your father would have shot first and didn't care to hear reasoning," Betty said.

"Really, Aunt Carol?" was all he said because I knew he was hurt.

"I loved you unconditionally when Justine died and I never treated you any different from my own child. It's more to what she is saying," she said.

"Loved me because I was my mother's child, or your beloved Justine's son?" He said. Again, she didn't respond. Turning to walk away, he paused and turned back around.

So I see Rodney didn't get it all from his father. And I thought my family was fucked up, but this has officially taken the cake.

***

"What in the Maury, you are not the father, fuckery they got going on? So they done stole the girl baby? That's some damn psychotic shit. Sis, you need to double check nothing else coming out the closet before you say I do. I thought our family had issues, baby, them Carter's a fool with it," Jasmine said laughing.

"Tell me about it, they got some shit going on with them," I said. "But enough of that, back to you and the story you was telling me last night before Landon made me get off the phone. What happened when Dom walked in the house? Since yo ass is still alive, that means he ain't kill you," I said to Jasmine. She had called me to tell me Mark had popped up at her house a few days ago, and Dominic's crazy ass walked in on his ass on the couch. Sis the only one I know that always finds herself in crazy ass situations. I mean I can't talk because the nigga I was talking to turnt out to be cousins with my baby daddy and shit, but still. Baby girl could never catch a break with Dom's ass. She had caught me in the middle of getting ready for work. Yes a bitch said work. Landon had finally agreed after much pleading and sucking dick until my jaws damn near fell off, I was finally allowed to start working in his clothing store as his manager. He needed one, and although he was getting better with walking, he wasn't nearly ready to stand on his feet that long yet.

"Bitch, I damn near peed on myself when I opened my eyes and his ass was standing there calm and shit holding his gun on Mark and talking to me at the same time," she said.

"I'm convinced Landon and Dom were dropped on their heads as a kid that's all. Both of their asses got issues," I chimed in.

"Girl who you telling, and that's not the fucking killing part. Instead of this nigga Mark keeping his fucking mouth closed because he got a gun on him, his stupid ugly ass had the nerve to say that he was there because I was carrying his seed," she said. I had to stop putting on my lashes and look down at the phone all crazy.

"I know you fucking lying! Like dead ass? I know Mark's square ass didn't tell this crazy ass fool with the gun some bullshit like that. Lawd, I'ma miss Mark, he was an idiot, but a damn good doctor. We need more black doctors. Whel, when is the funeral?" I said as I resumed beating my face. I knew without a doubt Dom pulled the trigger after that comment. It's just some shit you don't say, and that was definitely one of them.

"Girl he slapped his ass with the butt of the gun and told him if he still was there by the time he walked back to the living room, he was dead. Shit you would have thought Mark's ass went to school for track and field instead of medicine how his ass ran so fast out that damn house," she said as I killed myself laughing. I didn't condone violence, but Mark had Dom all the way fucked up for real. He better be grateful he didn't get shoot first fuck questions Dom.

"He lucky because I know he surely would have been dead if he'd ran into a nut case named Ghost. But fuck it, Mark said he wanted to catch a fade shout out to my nigga Lil Boosie," I said in my Nicki Minaj voice, still laughing.

"A lie. That nigga grew wings and flew out that bitch. Whatever he thought was gone happen, or whatever he rehearsed in his mind, that lick had him rethinking all of that shit," Jasmine said. After our laughter had died down, I went serious on her.

"So sis be honest, is there any truth to his allegations?" When she didn't immediately answer, my heart dropped. I knew how excited Dom was about this kid. Shit that's all he talked about. Jr. this, and Jr. that. I would hate for this to not be his son. I know for a fact this would crush him. Once I heard her sniffling, I knew the answer.

"Jas," I said.

"I honestly thought I was 100 percent certain that this was Dom's baby, Tommie. I haven't had sex with anybody else. I mean me and Mark hooked up before I left and came back home, but I could have sworn that was a week or two before I got back. My dates match up to the last time me and Dom had sex. In my heart I know Dom is the father, but I really don't know. I'm too far along for this bullshit, and been doing too damn good to let this break up apart. I'm just doing a pre paternity test on the baby. I can't wait another couple months. The suspense and wait would drive me crazy, on top of, I'm not tryna beef with my man that damn long. I thought he wouldn't stay at my house that night, but he did. I felt him get in bed with me a few hours later," she said sounding really sad and stressed out.

"Just like you was here for me during my situation with Landon and Rodney, and even when I said that slick shit and got put in the dog house, you stuck by my side. I'm not going anywhere. I'll get Landon to talk to Dom as well," I said.

"No the fuck you won't because I don't get in grown folks business, now get off the phone and hurry up. You know I run my legal businesses just like I run my illegal ones. I'ma dock your damn pay for being late," Landon snapped, walking into the room. He insisted on walking everywhere now even if it took him awhile to get there.

"Get her ass brother," I heard Jasmine saying through the phone laughing.

"You supposed to be on my side bitch," I said.

"Naw sis, you know what it is," he said.

"I'll hit you back later on sis. Love you," I said hanging up.

"You dock my pay and this pussy going into retirement," I said to him putting the finishing touches on my makeup. "And speaking of pay, I need my first raise tomorrow," I said laughing being funny.

"Damn it's like that huh?"

"Hell yeah. nigga what you thought? Shit fuck em, then I get some money," I said sticking my tongue out at him as I got up from my vanity. Reaching into his pocket, he pulled out a knot of money.

"Fuck him then you get some money huh? Okay this about 200 stacks, I was about to go cop a new whip, but now I think I'll see what a nigga can get for this shit?" He said with a raised eyebrow.

"Naw, I need to get my ass to work," I said laughing.

"Yo boss said you can be a few minutes late, so what's up. What freaky shit a nigga getting for this?" He said as he starting throwing money over my head. Shaking my head at his ass, I surely bent down and grabbed the money at the same time as I bounced my ass directly on his dick making before I walked to my closet and grabbed me a pair of shoes to go with my outfit.

"Damn really Tommie? That's how you coming? We doing it like that now? Fucking highway robbery bruh. I feel played on the cool," he said laughing. Coming out the closet in my shoes, he stopped laughing and just looked at me. I guess he hadn't really paid attention to what I was wearing until now.

"Nope, hell no. Take them jeans off. Ass sitting up just right. Matter of fact burn them hoes," he said.

"But bae these my favorite pair of fashion nova jeans," I pouted.

"Good, and some homeless person will put them to good use, but yo ass won't leave this house in them shits. Hell they got your hips looking good as fuck and I can see that ass from the front it's sitting up so fucking nice right now. Fuck. Okay, keep the jeans because they doing that body right right now. But you damn sure not wearing them to the store, not with the niggas that work there or shop there. I be done shut that whole fucking store down. Went in there and sprayed every fucking body," he said and I knew he was serious. Faking like I was mad, I rolled my eyes and walked back into my closet to find something else to wear. Taking my jeans off, I stood in the middle of our walk in closet in nothing but my button up shirt and a thong on.

"And you had a thong on as well. See now you just showing yo ass," I heard Landon say from behind me before he pushed me against the door. Before I could even register what had happened, he had hiked my leg up and slid deep inside of me.

"Fuck I can't enough of this pussy for some reason. Shit juicier then normal," he moaned as he pounded into me from behind. *Feels different because I'm pregnant*, I thought as I threw it back at him.

"I fucking love you girl," he said grabbed me by my throat and twisting my mouth around to him at the same time. Placing his lips on mines, we shared a long passionate kiss as he repeatedly hit my G-spot. I still hadn't told him I was pregnant, but I planned on revealing it really soon.

***

"Look what the cat drug in. It's good to see you Mr. Carter ," some guy said, walking up to us and dapping Landon up.

"Yeah, we missed you," some female said.

"If you need somebody to take care of you, or cook a meal or two, just let me know boss," another one said. I whipped my head in her direction so damn fast I almost caught whip lash. I know this lil' hoe didn't just try my entire life like this.

"Naw, I'm well taken care of. My wife makes sure I have everything I want and need," he said, putting her in her place. "Speaking of wife, this Tommie Knowles Carter, and she will be your new manager, so everyone needs to show her the same respect you show me. Samantha, I need you to show her the ropes like the cash register, and make sure she familiar with prices," Landon said to some girl. She already looked like she had a horrible attitude, so I hope she didn't have any issues because I wasn't gone take her shit. Gone was the timid quiet person I used to be. I done got a piece of bomb ass dick, and a taste of a real man, and done reinvented myself. The more I'm around Landon, the more I pick up his rude ass attitude, and don't give a shit mind frame.

"This permanently? Or just until you get better?" this hoe Samantha just had to say.

"Permanently. I was only working here until I found a manager, and since now I have, I'll only occasionally do pop ups. I expect business to still flow as usual, and rules to still apply. Y'all know I don't play, so keep that in mind just in case y'all try and get out of line so close to the holidays and find yourself without a job right before Christmas," Landon said. He had went from joking to serious in two point five seconds. Everyone knew he was serious too because they didn't crack not one smile.

"Nice to meet you all," I said waving. Damn nice to meet y'all? Really bitch, I scolded myself. I received a few dry "hey's" as a response. I wasn't particularly worried about if they liked me or not. At the end of the day, I wanted to prove to Landon I could do this job, and I deserved it, not because I was fucking the boss, but because I was good at what I did.

"Aye Terrance let me holla at you in the back," Landon said walking off. Being left alone with Samatha, and two other girls, I offered a smile as I walked behind the register.

"So how long you and boss man chilling? We didn't even know he had a girlfriend," Samantha said. I knew she was throwing shade, and I had to decide would I entertain her ugly ass, or keep it cute. Being that I was a boss, and this hoe was a worker, I decided that I would keep it cute and not stoop to her level, for now.

"You didn't know he had a girlfriend, because he doesn't have one," I said. "Now I'm not really familiar with a register, but if you show me one time, then I'll catch on. I pick up on things pretty quickly. Also, does Landon, I mean Mr. Carter have a book details prices of clothing? Or do you just go by whatever it rings up once it's scanned?" I asked her.

"So he not claiming you? Damn that's tough but don't feel bad, he probably for everybody," she said not even answering what I asked her. I see this hoe was really trying me. Raising my hand and displaying my bad ass, Auriya 18k engagement ring. My ring was absolutely gorgeous and those diamonds were most definitely dancing off the charts in it. I wasn't materialistic by a long shot, but one day Jasmine and I took it to get appraised just to see how much it cost. I figured he had spent about twenty thousand on it or something. The value of my ring was $547,247. My baby dropped half a mil on my ring and still told me I could have whatever I liked when it came to my wedding.

"See I said he doesn't have a girlfriend, because he has a soon to be wife. Now if we're done discussing that, can we get down to business?" I said shutting her ass down quick. The way her moth dropped open after seeing my ring was priceless. Yep I'm that bitch, and these hoes better know it.

***

"You ready to see granny?" I asked Royalty as we got out of the car, and walked up the steps to the facility that my mom was currently living in for cancer rehabilitation patients. Last time I was here, her doctors said she was progressing fine, and that made me feel better, and gave me hope. At this point, since hope, faith, and prayer was all I had to rely on given her situated, I accepted all the hope faith and prayer that I could get. Walking into her room, I noticed her laying on the bed watching. Steve Harvey's Family Feud.

"Hey momma." I said walking over to a chair and sitting down. Sitting up, and stretched her hands out, and I got up to give her a hug until she closed her arms.

"Not you girl, give me my grandbaby ," she said bursting my little bubble all the way.

"Well excuse me," I said laughing as I handed Royalty over. She was dressed up today in a shirt long sleeve onesie shirt that said Daddy's Angel that also had gold polka dots on it. I paired the shirt with some pink tights, and a black tutu.

"What is your momma feeding you? She so big and juicy," my momma said.

"I feed her bottles, but everybody else feeds her big tail everything else," I said laughing because my baby was chunky with her little fat legs. She wasn't over weight or anything, she was just healthy.

"How everything been going since we last talked, baby?"

"Everything been good ma," I lied but I didn't need her stressing over anything I had going on, or Landon and his Oprah worthy family issues. She needed to focus all of her energy on her own situation.

"I had dreams about fish last night, so either you're pregnant, or I must want some fish," she said.

"Yes, I'm pregnant," I said after a long pause. I might as well go ahead and tell her because I can't hide once my stomach gets bigger. It was already hard enough hiding it now. Pretty soon, wearing a bigger size shirt wouldn't cut it anymore.

"Just sliding them on out, huh?" She said.

"Dang ma," I relied laughing at her choice of words. We spent the rest of the visit just laughing at talking like nothing in the world was wrong. These are the days I lived for, and the ones I would always cherish.

CHAPTER 11
I'M BUILT FOR THIS SHIT, SO COME HARDER THAN THAT....

DOM

Looking at the numbers for the month, I knew I had to do better. I was letting the problems I was having affect my damn bread, and that shit wasn't gone fly with me. Jasmine walked into the kitchen, and grabbed some orange juice out of the refrigerator, and I pretended I didn't even see her ass as I continued going over the numbers from my trap. I would just have to replace the shit because I didn't feel like hearing Ghost's mouth about how I'm running shit, and I definitely would pop Menace's old ass if he came at me left about some bread. It's my fuck up, so I was gone suck that shit up and put the money back.

"When are you going to talk to me Dominic?" Jasmine said to me. Still, I didn't say shit to her. I wasn't ready to deal with that shit. When I was with Jackie and she told me she was pregnant, that was the best news I'd gotten my entire life. I changed my whole life around the moment she told me those words. I started making plans to get more money, and elevated in these streets so my family could be straight. That's right before me and Ghost hooked up with Menace. Then when she overdosed and lost my baby, my world felt like it ended that day. Here comes Jasmine telling me she's pregnant, and I felt like I was given a second chance to be a father again. But, like a thief in the night, a nigga was once again robbed of that feeling. It's crazy because despite knowing it could be Mark's baby, I still loved that baby with everything in me. I finally see what Ghost meant when he said Royalty was his baby regardless of what happened with him and Tommie. However, even though I still loved the lil' nigga growing in her stomach, a nigga didn't know how to properly deal with all the emotions I was feeling. I felt weak and like a sucker for still loving her hot pussy ass, and the baby. Until I worked out these feelings, I just wasn't fucking with her.

"When I get ready to," I said to her as I grabbed my paperwork, put it back inside the folder, grabbed my phone, keys and walked out the door. I was gone stop by to see Jacinta before I went to help Julius and Synthia at Fly Guys.

***

POW!POW!

Letting off two rounds into the niggas in front of me, I turned to the ones to my side. I had a short fuse lately dealing with all of this Jasmine and Mark bullshit. I'm surprised that even though I wasn't fucking with her, my black ass still was at her shit every night like I didn't have my own crib. Hell, my shit was way bigger than hers, and my bed was more comfortable, but yet in still I took my ass to her shit every night. I don't know if it's because I wanted to make sure Mark wasn't there, or because a nigga couldn't sleep without her. Combine that with the fact that we still haven't found out who tried to off my brother, who sent the fucking lips to his crib, and who shot up Fly Guy, had me on edge. We popped the nigga Rodney, but shit was still happening, which meant maybe his ass wasn't behind all this shit, just some of it. Come to think of it, shit didn't go left until I snatched Jackie from that crack house. Then my shit got shot up. But, that was only hours apart though, so there was no way dude could have set that up in that short amount of time. They had to have been casing that place out. And, before we killed dude, he said some bitch hired him. Thinking long and hard, I knew a trip to Atlanta was needed. I needed to find out more information about who this bitch was, and the streets was already talking. Hell, if they didn't talk, I'd bleed the entire city red until somebody told me something. At this point, the wrong word literally wrong word or move would get you popped. I was on ten and didn't plan on coming down anytime soon.

"So tell me again why I sent y'all to do a job, and y'all came back empty handed?" I asked pointing my gun at Don and Trek. I had sent them along with the other two niggas I just bodied, out in the hood to follow a lead on this Ghost situation.

"We did get some news boss. Word on the street is a bitch is the one who ran down on Ghost. Tron off 15th, ol lady said she was on the highway when the shit happened. Said olegirl bussed off in the car and took off running. We was going back over there today to get her to give us a description of the bitch," Don said not even flinching at the fact I had a gun in his face. Lil' nigga was only 18 and had heart unlike Trek's ass. The nigga was 22, and was shaking so fucking hard, he just about bout peed on his damn self

"Well them niggas should have spoken up faster before I started shooting then. Call the clean up crew to come get they asses off the floor, then get y'all ass back out there and see what the fuck she got to say," I said. "And Trek tighten your bitch ass up before you be six feet under. Damn heart bout to jump out yo chest, ol' scary ass." Turning to look at Justice and his crew, before I could even get a word out, he beat me to it.

"My bitches done damn near ran through all his hoes. Beating them bitches on sight every fucking day. Them some tough ass hoes. Don't matter how many ass whoopings they get, still get back out on the corner that night, or next day. Still ain't seen no sign of him though," Justice said. Nodding my head at him, I looked up to see Ghost walking inside. I can't even lie and say I wasn't happy as hell to see him. I hope like hell he was coming back to work as well because this shit was getting to be too much. I don't know how the nigga did it. Making sure the books straight, keeping these niggas in line, dealing with the baby momma shit, and tryna find out who tryna get at us was just too fucking much for my ass. It made me appreciate my position in this business even more. I let Ghost handle all this shit, and I was just there when it was time to push a nigga shit back, or check on the traps.

"Nigga, what yo cripple ass doing here?" I said laughing as I walked and dapped him up.

"Y'all asses can get back to work," I said to the men.

"I see your ass in this bitch thinking you the boss and shit," Ghost said, referrring to the two bodies on the floor.

"Man fuck them niggas, but I prolly did pop their asses without listening to what they had to say. My bad," I said shrugging my shoulders.

"Nigga, yo ass always been trigger happy, and I always told you that shit gone be the death of you. Think before you react. Every situation doesn't need to be handled with a bullet." Ghost said. Nigga was always tryna drop wisdom and shit. I mean in this situation he was right because they did die for nothing, but I for damn show wasn't admitting that shit to him.

"What's good dog? How you feeling though, real talk?" I asked him as the clean-up crew got them niggas together to go dispose of their bodies.

"Shit not a hundred percent better, but I ain't got time to still be laying around. Not with how crazy shit gettin in these streets. Then with the shit that I found out the other day, nigga need to take a vacation some damn where," he said running his hands down his face.

"Shit what you found out? You got a bitch pregnant?" I said, laughing.

"Only shit I'm slidin in raw is my girl, you got me fucked up. Everybody don't hit ugly hoes naked like you. You still burning?" He said referring to a bitch I hit a few years ago after the club. I had a jimmy on, it broke and I was too fucked up to stop.

"Remind me not to tell your Sponge Bob Square pants looking ass shit else. You not I'm sensitive about that." I said.

"Fuck yo cry baby ass, but man this shit fucked a nigga head up. So how bout Nurse Betty is a nigga's Tlady."

"Nigga get the fuck out of here... Nurse Betty ya moms? Damn and I sure was thinking about knocking her old ass down. She got some ass to be an old lady," I said, laughing.

"If I knew it wouldn't hurt my sister, I'd pop your ass," Ghost said. Nigga was big mad.

"Fuck you, ol' cry baby ass nigga," I said throwing his words right back at him. "And we both gone be dead because even if I catch a few bullets, I'm still bussing back," I said.

"Shit you won't bounce back from these bullets," he said raising his shirt revealing his desert eagle. That bitch did spit out big ass bullets.

"Man I'll haunt the fuck out of your ass. If I can't ever get pussy anymore, you won't either. Every time you try and get some ass, I'm blocking. Ima be in that bitch tormenting the shit out your ass," I said laughing.

"You stupid as fuck," he said, laughing. "But check it, I also caught a break in the case. The FBI agent I got on payroll finally got back to me with that informant."

"We already know it's Vivian's bald mouth ass. She not a threat since somebody got to her ass before we could. Ugly scarecrow-looking bitch. I never liked that hoe," I said.

"That's the part that blew my mind though bruh, I didn't read her name on none of the paperwork, and I was fucking positive it was that hoe," he said pulling a folder out from under his arms that I just noticed was there. Taking the folder from him, I opened the shit up. In the folder it detailed how a Vanessa Caldwell had been their personal informant with supplying them with evidence against me Ghost, and all of our men, including Menace. Crazy part about all this shit was that the dates she gave went way back to before we was even running shit.

"Who the fuck is Vanessa?" I asked.

"That's not even the crazy part, did you peep the last name?" Ghost asked me. Looking down at the name again, it wasn't registering to me.

"What I'm missing?" I asked him.

"Menace's wife, Vivian's maiden name is Caldwell," he said.

"Shit sounding too fucking suspect by the minute. We need to hit Menace ass up and see what the fuck is up," I said.

"He should be pulling up soon. It's time to get to the bottom of this shit," Ghost said.

"Man before he get here, I gotta run some shit by you," I said running my hands down my face. I had been avoiding this conversation for a minute, throwing myself in my work to keep from thinking about it. But, the shit was really fucking with me.

"Don't go all serious on me. I guess it's story time since I just told you about my situation, so what's up? Crackhead Jackie got you on that shit? A bitch burnt you again, and now you gotta get your dick cut off?" Ghost said, shooting dumb ass question after dumb ass question out at me.

"Really fool? Where the hell do you even come up with this shit at though?" I asked him as I burst out laughing.

"Well hell, I'm tryna see what's wrong with your funny looking ass. So nigga, just say it. Spit that shit out," he said pulling a blunt out of his pocket.

"Didn't Tommie say you couldn't smoke shit until you was walking fine again?" I said.

"Fuck Tommie, dick runs my household," he said firing it up. Pulling my phone out, I pretended to dial Tommie's number.

"Aye Tommie you know Ghost," was all I got to say before this nigga damn near broke my hand, trying to snatch my phone from me. Laughing, I said,

"Thought Tommie don't run shit though?" I said laughing.

"Fuck you," he said laughing. "What's up though seriously?" Smile immediately leaving my face, I got serious as I ran my hands down my face again.

"Spit it out," he said.

"Damn give me time, shit," I said. "Jasmine pregnant," I started.

"Nigga you been hitting that bad weed again? Shit, we been knew Jas was pregnant. Nigga, yo ass had me thinking it was something serious-,"

"By either me or Mark," I said finishing up what I was gone say. The look on his face said it all, he was just as shocked as I was.

"Nigga get the fuck out of here with that shit," He said.

"I swear."

"Put that on something," Ghost said.

"I put that on Dominique," I said calling out the name of my baby girl that Jackie had killed by overdosing on drugs. He knew I was serious because.

"How you found out?"

"Shit I walked in her crib, and this nigga had his feet propped up like shit was sweet."

"Well since the nigga dead, you ain't got shit to worry about," Ghost said.

"Naw, I ain't kill his ass." I said. His eyes got buck before he got up from his chair and walked over to me placing the back of his hands on my head like I was Royalty or something, and he was checking her temperature. Swatting his hand away, I said,

"Nigga what the hell is you doing?"

"Shit I'm tryna make sure yo ass ain't coming down with nothing. You mean to tell me you just killed these fools like it was nothing, but this nigga still breathing. Did you at least beat his ass?"

"Naw, but I slapped him with the gun," I said, now semi-embarrassed that I didn't do shit to this nigga.

"Man you can't be out here hanging with me and letting niggas punk you in yo shit. Especially square ass niggas. Hell, no wonder niggas been trying ya left and right so much. Let's go beat his ass at least if you don't want to kill the nigga. Barely walking and all, I'm still putting niggas to sleep with these bitches," Ghost said, holding both his fists up.

"Nigga fuck you mean ion need to help to throw these bitches. I let his square ass make it because that'll only bring more heat our way. You was the main one just talking about think before I react," I said throwing his words back at him. "That's not what I wanted to talk to you about. I love Jr regardless if he mine or not, but how do I make myself not feeling as though I'm looking like I'm pulling some ol' sucker for love type shit by raising another nigga seed?" I asked, because the shit was really fucking with me.

"Shit anybody who knows me knows you can't be sucker and Ghost in the same sentence. These hoes know I don't trick money on them, and before Tommie, they couldn't get nothing but this dick. So it's not about what it looks like, and fuck feelings. You love that baby, then love that baby period. It's no different than you getting with a chick with a kid. If you love her, then you love anything that comes from her, the rest is dead game. That ain't no sucker shit, that's some real grown man shit. Any bitch ass nigga can fuck a girl and get her pregnant, but it takes a real man to raise a child. Once you make up in your mind that's your kid, the rest don't fucking matter. Shit, everybody and they mammy know how I feel about Royalty. To the point they forgot she wasn't biologically mines. That's my princess and I wish a bitch or nigga would try and tell me different, because you already know I'ma see about that. Tommie can go before my baby ever will. Hell even if we co-parent, Royalty leaving my house going to stay somewhere else is dead. Tommie's ass better build a wing into the house or move into the guest room," he said and his crazy throwed-off ass was serious as fuck. But, he made a lot of sense. I loved my son already, and was excited for his birth, and that's the end of that. Even if Mark was the father, him taking my son was dead game, his ass could take a bullet instead. Shit *my* son, I liked the sound of that.

Love & Hennessy 4

CHAPTER 12

SHIT STARTING TO MAKE SENSE…..

GHOST

Menace had perfect timing because soon as we wrapped our conversation up, the doors to the warehouse opened, and he walked inside. At one point we were father and son close, but shit with everything going on with this fed case, and me seeing his car pulling up at the spot, it had left us in a bad spot. Walking over and dapping me and Dom out, he sat down, and I cut straight to the chase.

"Aye, the reason I got at you that day at my crib was because I hired the FBI agent to keep me up on game about this case going on. Shit, long story short, he told me the case was built solely off information from a confidential informant. Well he told me the meeting place and shit with the CI, so shit I just wanted to see who it was, so I rolled out there. Imagine my surprise when your car came rolling up. Now given light of everything I found out, I now know it wasn't you."

"Shit I could have saved you all the trouble and told your ass that. The fuck I look like turning snitch? The feds haven't been able to build a case to make stick against me all this time. And don't think it wasn't for lack of trying. How many niggas you know live to be old, retired, and filthy rich having made it out the game without having to do some major time? The feds couldn't fuck with me even if they tried to fuck with me. Shit I knew it was something with you, but I for damn show wasn't gone try and reason with your young and dumb ass. I was gone let you come to that conclusion on your fucking own. I did have to put you on your ass, though," he said.

"Nigga I got with your old ass, fuck you talking about."

"Shit, son you dreaming. Them fucking meds you on got you hallucinating. I was fucking you up. If my baby girl hadn't been there, you would have gotten your ass handed to you."

"See I didn't want to say shit, but yo eye was sitting on swole," Dom said being messy as he started laughing.

"Fuck all that. you just ain't beat a nigga ass. You did get a few good licks in, but shit I rocked off on your ass a bunch too. I ain't wanna hurt your old ass, just wanted you to feel that pressure," I said. I felt kinda played on the cool, but I wouldn't dwell on that right now.

"Yeah you got a few good ones, I'll give you that. Back to this CI. If you found out it wasn't me, then who was it?" Menace said.

"Vivian," I said.

"Get the fuck out of here," he said.

"Shit unless somebody else rolling around the city with a customized black Rolls Royce with personalized plates," I said. Putting his hand on his chin, he said.

"And when this was?"

"The night my daughter was born. That's why I didn't get a look at the face. Dom called to tell me Tommie was in labor, and those few seconds I looked away, the meeting was over."

"Well then it couldn't have been her. The night Royalty was born, we were on my yacht trying to have a peaceful night. I had been trying to leave her for awhile, but she had been acting right lately, so I took her on a date out at the sea. That's why it took us to long to make it to the hospital. We were at least two hours out to sea," he said.

"She could have met up with them and came back before you noticed her gone," Dom said and I pointed at him signaling I agreed.

"Again, it takes two hours to get to land, and the entire time we were there, she was full of dick, or sleep. Shit I would let her rest up a bit before I fucked her back to sleep again. And I never went to sleep if that's your next question. Trust me she ain't leave that fucking bed," he said.

"Damn ain't you too fucking old for that shit?" Dom said laughing.

"Shit you better ask your momma about this dick, it's the truth." Menace said.

"Damn pops you got that too?" I said, slapping him high five. I'm sure he didn't but Dom's Tlady was bad as fuck. I accidentally knocked that down a few years back.

"Fuck both of y'all," Dom said laughing.

"Man, anyways back to business. Who is Vanessa to your wife? Because her name is over all of the CI paperwork? She could have been the driver, but how did she get your car?" I asked.

"You sure it was my car?" He said.

"As much as I've eyeballed that car and even went bought one just like it, I for damn sure know it's yours." I said. A weird look flashed across his face causing him to jump up quickly. As he walked swiftly towards the door, I said.

"Aye, wait. Who is the bitch?" I asked.

"Her twin sister," he said exiting the warehouse.

"Twin?" I repeated.

"So there's two of their asses? Damn I hope they not identical because that would just be a waste. Two ugly ass people with the same face," this stupid nigga said. Shit left me more confused than ever at this point though.

***

"Aye. bust this right real quick," I told my driver. I was on my way home, and being the observant nigga that I was, I saw a car tailing us.

"Debo behind us?" I asked Chico one of my body guards, who immediately got on the phone.

"Where you at?" Chico spoke into the phone. "Alright," he said hanging up.

"Debo said he behind the car, you want him to light that bitch up?" Chico said.

"Naw, park right there and see what their asses do. I'm tired of this fucking cat and mouse game. If they wanted a nigga head, then fuck it. Let's do this right here right now. Nigga just want to live in peace, raise my child, and marry my girl, that's it," I said pulling my gun out of my waist. Pulling into the parking lot of a Wendy's, I looked out the window as the car sped past us. I almost looked away until I caught a glimpse of the driver. *Well I'll be damned*, I thought to myself. I just know that ain't who been tryna get at me. Shit it all makes sense if it was, but damn really though.

"You want us to follow the car?" Chico said to me.

"Naw, I'ma personally handle this one," I said. "Drive me to the crib, and make sure we don't have anymore unwanted company. Hit a few blocks, make a few wrong turns and shit," I said sitting back in the seat. Once we made it home, I walked inside of a dark and quiet house, and immediately became alarmed.

"Tommie?Mariah? Betty?" I called out. When I didn't get a response for anybody, I pulled my gun out and held it in front of me as I walked slowly up the stairs. Once I made it to the first floor landing, I saw rose petals trailing from the beginning of the stairs leading to my room at the end of the hallway. Still, I kept my gun out. "Tommie?" I said again. Reaching my room, I slowly opened the door to see Tommie, laying inside of our bed covered in whip scream, strawberries and caramel. Walking further into the room and kicking the door closed, I walked over to the bed and looked down at her.

"Woman, what are you doing?" I asked her and I ran my finger over some of the cream and placed it in my mouth."

"Giving you a late night snack," she said. Smirking, I walked into the bathroom and grabbed a few paper towels off the paper towel holder, and walked back into the room. Sitting up slightly, she said,

"Bae what you doing with those towels?"

"I'm about to eat my snack, shit I'm not tryna get messy. Now lay down and feed me that pussy," I said and she quickly giggled and laid back down. This is why she deserved that rock I put on her finger. She had a way of making the troubles of the day disappear. I had intentions on coming home, and showering before I went and paid my little friend a visit, but seeing what I came home to, that most definitely could wait.

***

"So I was thinking rose gold, pale pink, and cream for wedding colors," the wedding coordinator said. "The bride says she's picked out her dress, so don't forget to get fitted for your tux with her groomsmen. I still wish you hadn't insisted on canceling your venue date and moving the wedding up to a month. The spring wedding would have been fabulous."

"You're fucking right I don't want to wait until the spring," I said.

"I really had my mind set on a spring wedding though," Tommie said.

"Well, unset your mind. It's nothing wrong with a summer wedding. Both times will be hot as hell anyway. I don't even care about a big wedding, we could get married tomorrow at the justice of the peace, shit. Won't make no difference," I said ready to fucking go. I can't believe I let Tommie's ass convince me to come to this bullshit. I told her my involvement is strictly check writer and card swiper.

"I'm only getting married once Landon, so it's very important to me. If I can't have it in the spring, I at least want a nice wedding. But those colors are amazing, I think they will pop just right together. I'd also like a little shimmery gold in there as well," Tommie said.

"It's your world baby, whatever you want," I said to her.

"Great, now that's all settled, I'll get right on that. Now Ms. Knowles you did mention that you wanted real imported flowers in that correct?" The coordinator asked, looking at paper that I'm guessing Tommie filled out.

"Yes," Tommie said.

"Great, I think the flowers will still go great regardless if it's spring or not. Now I did price some and I received a good quote," she said. Just as her assistant walked in and offered us some water. Accepting the water, I was in the middle of taking a sip when she said,

"I have a price of 14,452 that I can lock in today." I damn near choked on my water when I heard that bullshit.

"14 grand for some damn flowers?" I said.

"Baby they are imported and real. I have to have them," Tommie said.

"If you don't go to Walmart and get some flowers and quit fucking play girl," I said to her. Poking her lip out, she looked at me with a face.

"But baby, you said I could have whatever I liked," Tommie said.

"It's a good price on the flowers, but you guys can think it over, just don't take too long because the deal might leave," Jennifer, our wedding coordinator said.

"Yeah we'll have to think about it. I said whatever you like but within reason. I'm not paying 14 grand for some fucking flowers," I said standing firm in what the fuck I said. This whole wedding shit was getting ridiculous by the minute. I knew women went all out, but damn I created a monster, and it probably was only going to get worse.

***

I've been looking at Aunt Carol funny since everything popped off, to the point where I got her ass a hotel room for her safety. Shit with the mind frame that I had right now combined with the fact that I had to dead her snake ass son, I was likely to pop her old ass. And honestly through all of what I found out, I still loved her, and It would cut me deep to have to bury her. Regardless of the circumstances, when ma dukes, well Justine died, Aunt Carol took a nigga in and raised me like her own. She worked two jobs just to put a little food in the house and clothes on our backs, and she never complained not once. She'd be bone tired from working one job, and would still come home, cook us breakfast, shower, and go immediately to her second job. The real definition of a hard-working, strong, African queen. I just couldn't see this vindictive side, but now that I knew she was capable of it, I wasn't putting anything past her. It did make me question a lot of things in regards to shit that's happened in the past and present, like could she have something to do with that shit? She had been blowing a nigga line up all day, so I decided to give in and agree to have lunch with her one on one, just to hear her out, and get a better understanding of the situation, if I could. Walking inside of the Cheesecake Factory, I looked around until I spotted her.

"Welcome to the Cheesecake Factory sir, how many will it be this afternoon?" The hostess said, eyeing a nigga like I was a piece of steak. Shaking my head at her, I just walked off headed towards where Aunt Carol was. Taking a seat, I immediately picked up the drink menu, because I needed a double shot of something, anything, to get me through this lunch. Once I placed my order with the server, and took me a drink of water, I said,

"So you asked me here just to look at me? What's up? You have the answers I need, so let's not beat around the bush," I said not bothering to sugar coat shit, or play nice. I didn't have time for this shit, and I needed to know was she the vile devil in sheeps clothing that Betty made her out to be. Taking a deep breath, she begin from the beginning explaining to me her version of the story, which didn't sound much different from what Betty said. Just sounds like it was told from a more bitter, spiteful point of view, but still I continued to listen anyway because I needed this closure to accept the fact that the sweet old lady who I would give my life for, wasn't as sweet and innocent as I had believed. They say the devil comes in all forms, shapes and sizes, and now I was starting to believe that saying. It really cut me to the core because she was the last family I had left since I had to off Rodney's ass. No matter that Nurse Betty birthed me and really wanted me or not, this was my real family staring across from me right now. Even though she did right by me as a kid, she was no longer welcome around my family, because although she was my last blood relative, Royalty and Tommie were my life and new family. I'd never risk anything happening to them, no matter what.

CHAPTER 13

TIME TO PUT THINGS INTO MOTION...

KELINA

"It's time to put this fucking plan into motion. The longer we wait, the more fucking money a nigga missing. Janae, one of my hoes, hit me up and said some bitches jumping on them every fucking day. Ever block they move to, them hoes there. They know a nigga don't give a fuck about no fucked up face, hell they won't stop somebody from wanting their dick sucked. Still, shit fucking with my business. This shit got Dom's name written all over it," Kenneth said, going on and on about the shit.

"Nigga shut the fuck up or kill the nigga. You been on this same shit for a few days now damn. You wanna roll by there and see what's up? Hell I though that would have been the first thing you did when we touched down," I said to him. I couldn't stand a fake ass thug like him. Talking all this raw shit, but won't bust a grape. He was one those barking ass but no biting ass niggas.

"Shit, I'm naked right now." he said. Reaching under my seat, I grabbed a gun and tossed it to him.

"Here you go. We can go over and check shit out."

"Who you supposed to be, bruh? GI Jane or some shit? And I know they probably got a gang of niggas guarding that bitch just waiting on a nigga to step into they weak ass trap. Gotta come harder than that." On one hand knowing Ghost and Dom, he probably was right. But, shit still sounded soft as hell to me. Spotting the car I was waiting on, I turned off onto the highway making sure to keep a good distance behind the car.

"You think this gone finally lead us to his house?" Kenneth said.

"It should, or at least lead us to somewhere promising, like a stash house we can hit," I said keeping up with the black SUV that Ghost was in. I wanted to take anything he loved away, and it was nothing he loved more than money. You made sure Amber and Chelsea all set for their part?" I asked him. We were sending Amber on a duck ass suicide mission, and honestly, we were banking on her getting her stupid ass killed.

"Yeah, they gon' be the perfect distraction for us to snatch the child. I know Amber's ass like the back of my hand, she not bright enough to know her part is a trap, to get her killed. Shit while they off killing her, we can get the money and the baby. Shit we need to snatch Tommie and Jasmine's ass. You know that would double our money," he said but his was wants fooling nobody. He really wanted to snatch Jasmine because he thought he could charm her out the panties, and put her on his team. He really thought to highly of his damn self, because the nigga wasn't even popping like that, but you couldn't tell him shit.

"We don't have enough man power to snatch everybody, Vanessa's ass off tryna get that money out of Menace, and kill him, so shit that leaves just us. We can't start changing the plan right now, we need everything to run smoothly," I said, noticing the SUV pulling over into a burger joint, but nobody got out.

"Shit,I think they might have caught on to us following them," I said.

"Quick, buss that right," Kenneth said.

"Nigga, we can't fucking panic. If they have caught on to us, they probably got guns and everything ready to blast our asses," I said.

"It's daylight, he can't do shit," Kenneth said.

"You bought a dumb ass nigga. You think Ghost give a damn that it's daylight? That nigga will pop yo ass outside a police station," I said, cruising by their parked car casually. "We'll wait until later on tonight, and swing by the spot to check on yo hoes," I said once we had gotten a good distance from them. It wasn't them I was scared of, but shit, I damn sure wasn't dumb by a long shot. I couldn't go into battle with one damn gun. I knew at this point it was too risky to swing back around and still try and follow them home, so I kept driving.

***

"Be quiet, stupid," I said as we worked our way into one of the stash houses I knew about from the small time Ghost had allowed me into his world. Things were moving along as planned in our plot to take down Ghost as his crew, and I was ready to check mate this game we were planing. But first, I needed every dime I could fucking get, because if this plan to kill the whole crew didn't work out, I could still disappear and live comfortably.

"You expect a nigga to be Spider-Man or some shit? Does it look like I'm the type to climb any damn where?" Kenneth asked me. I don't know why the fuck I ever brought him along with me. Every since we hatched our plan, the nigga been stuck to me like glue like Ima double cross his ass or some shit. Well, that's exactly what the fuck my ass would do given the chance. Finally making it to a window, that I knew didn't lock, I lifted it up and climbed inside, and he followed after me. Tiptoeing over to the door, I opened it and slowly walked out into the hallway of the two story home they used as one of their stash houses.

"What the fuck is that smell?" Kenneth asked me failing miserably at whispering. To be so damn scary, the nigga sholl had a way of acting like he was harder than he actually was. If somebody buss out of one of these rooms right now, I know his was would piss on himself. The further we walked down the hallway, the worse the smell became to the point where I almost throw up in my mouth.

"I don't know, but we have to get this money tonight," I said. Slowly creeping down the stairs, I noticed shit didn't look like it did the last time I was here.

"You sure this the stash house and not some junky crack house? This nigga keep money in this dump? Hell, even my hoes living better than this," Kenneth said.

"Yes I'm sure, they might have just changed a few things," I whispered back as I made it to the living room area. Where there was once a table stacked to the ceiling with money, there was now nothing.

"So, where this money at?" Kenneth said?

"Maybe in that room," I said pointing to a door off to the side by the living room. Opening it up, we were met with nothing but piles and piles of dead bodies. Guess we found the source of the stench.

"Yeah, this is a stash house alright, them niggas just stashing bodies instead of cash," Kennth said walking over to one of the bodies and sticking his hands in the pants pocket.

"What you doing?" I asked him.

"Shit, running these fools pockets. I don't see a nigga like Ghost killing somebody then taking they wallet, he said as he pulled out a stack of hundreds. "Bingo," he said. As sick as the shit sounded, he had a point. With about fifty bodies on here, I figured we could still come up on a small fortune. Guess this wasn't a wasted trip after all.

CHAPTER 14
TRYING TO FIX WHAT'S BROKEN….

JASMINE

"What do you guys mean she's gone?" I said loudly. "Who signed off on that because I wasn't called, and I know my father wouldn't do that without talking to me first. My mother hasn't woken up since she's been here, therefore nobody authorized you to move my fucking mother, and she is not back in the fucking hospital by sundown, this will be a free clinic when I get done with y'all asses," I yelled. With everything going on with Dominic, combined with me working more to take my mind off my situation, I hadn't gotten up here to see my mother in awhile, but I knew my father had been visiting her, and I was still updated via the nurses on her condition periodically. I had stopped by today with flowers to see her before I met Tommie, and they just told me she was moved, but couldn't specifically tell me why. I was so mad at them, and at myself that I didn't know what to do. This was mostly my fault for going from seeing her daily, or missing a few visits. I would never forgive myself or Dominic if something happened to her. Feeling my side throbbing, I turned and walked out of the hospital and got into my car breathing heavily. I had to get breathing under control, and heartbeat steady. I was all fucked up, and again I blamed Dominic. It was going on a month, and Dom still wasn't really speaking to me. He really had me fucked up at this pony because my ass couldn't even get no damn dick. I was starting to see how Tommie felt when she was walking around miserable and horny as hell. I swear if push comes to shove, I'm raping this nigga tonight. Then he had to nerve to come to my house every night, shower, and get inside my end with nothing but some boxers on looking like a delicious snack. Last night, he slept naked and I almost lost my damn mind. Starting up my car after a few minutes, I pulled off to meet with Tommie and the wedding planner. I would be glad when this wedding was over because her ass has officially taken the term bridezilla to a whole new level. Ghost had really messed up when he told her spoiled ass that she could have whatever she liked, because she took those words to heart.

***

"Are you even listening to me Jas?" Tommie said. Me, her, and Royalty along with our body guards were all out shopping. We had just left going over wedding things with Jennifer, and decided to do some shopping before she headed to check on the store. I was so proud of her. My baby was a mother, soon to be wife, and working woman now. I had popped up at her job one day, and she was really doing the damn thing. My baby had matured right before my eyes, and as her maid of honor and big sister, I couldn't be happier.

"What you said?" I asked her.

"I said I wanted to show you this husband and wife dance, and do you think Landon will do it with me? Also, I want my bridal court to do a little dance for him. I was thinking Destiny Child Cater 2 you? What you think?" She asked me handing me her phone. The minute I clicked on the video, I knew Ghost wasn't going for that. The next video, was of three bridesmaids and the bride dancing to Cater 2 you by Destiny Child. It was a very cute routine, but my big ass just couldn't do it.

"Now you know Ghost isn't the type to do no shit like this. Girl, bye. That's video you showed me they was hitting the stanky leg and all. You'll be lucky if you get a first dance out of his ass. The second video was cute, but I'm trying to figure out how do you propose my big ass doing the moves exactly? Because if you hadn't noticed, one of us is big pregnant and uncomfortable," I said spotting an Auntie Anne's and having a sudden craving for a pepperoni pretzel.

"Let's stop by the pretzel place real quick," I said not even waiting for a response as I headed over.

"No one of us is big, I'm just not uncomfortable yet," she said. Not sure what she meant by that, I placed my order, got my pretzel, and dig in. Once I had taken a few bites, I waited for her to get hers. Once we were back headed towards Carters, a children's store. Before we could even make it to the store, I saw Kenneth and some bitch walking towards us. *Lawd here we go again with this stalking ass nigga. I'm glad I never gave him this ass, because he would really be a class A* stalker, I thought to myself. But being nice, I said,

"Hey, Kenneth."

"Sup ma." He said to Tommie, who hit him with a head nod. Bending down to the stroller, he went to speak to Royalty, but Tommie jerked the stroller from me so fast I thought it was on fire.

"Damn, bitch what's up?" I asked giving her the side eye.

"I don't know this nigga, and he don't need to be all in my baby face like that so the security can go tell Landon, and he kill all of us. Shit no thank you, I can't afford to die today shit I been working overtime, so I'm looking forward to payday," she said just as Big Rick walked up.

"Everything alright over here?" He said making sure his gun was visible. Throwing his hands up in surrender, Kenneth said,

"It's all good man. I just got back in town speaking to an old friend is all. I'll get out of you ladies' hair, y'all enjoy your shopping day," he said winking as he walked off.

"That nigga is hella fucking strange," Tommie said as we headed towards the entrance of Carters. Walking in, she begin looking through little girls clothes. I said,

"Now like I was saying, this dance isn't pregnant friendly sis. I think doing a dance with your bridal party is cool, just a pregnant friendly dance."

"I'm going to be doing the dance too Jas," she said thumbing through the clothes. "You think this cute?" She asked me holding up the ugliest shirt ever.

"You know that shit not cute, don't play my niece like that. Ain't that right Royalty?" I said, leaning down inside the tricked out stroller Ghost got her. He's the only person I know that complains about buying real flowers, but spent almost 20 thousand on this custom-made stroller for his princess, Royalty. I just know wherever he gets a son, that's kid will be fresh and fly as hell. Speaking of sons, I was patiently waiting for the prenatal paternity results to come back. They should be in today or tomorrow. I knew in my heart that Dom was the father, but I couldn't be too sure, and that was killing me.

"I feel like my baby so cute that she can make ugly weird shit look bomb as hell. I know my son will be just as cute," she said.

"Wait what? You pregnant?" I asked her.

"Shit about time your slow ass caught on to these hints I've been dropping. To be so smart, you so ditzy Jasmine," she said laughing.

"Damn little house on the praise, let me drop one before you start shooting them out back to back. And what happened to, "fuck what Landon talking about I'm not having another baby right now because that shit hurt?" " I said.

"She betrayed me," she said, patting her pants in the crotch area. I couldn't do shit but laugh.

"Well I'm happy for you. Are you ready for two kids though? I know Ghost ass was beyond excited so I won't even ask how he took the news."

"I haven't told him yet. You are the first one I've told. I'm going to see momma at the end of the day with Royalty, and I'll tell her."

"Why haven't you told him?" I asked her with my eyebrows raised.

"It's nothing like that, I'm not having doubts, I just wanted to know the sex first. My doctor said on my next visit they should be able to tell me. I wanted to surprise him with his son. That's my wedding gift to him," she said.

"Well yeah he'll love it," I said. "You guys have come a long way. From the break up, to the Rodney situation, to Kelina, and now y'all getting married. I see growth in both of you guys and I'm proud of you. If only I can get my situation together. I feel like I'm being punished for something I didn't intentionally do. I didn't cheat on this man or anything. It's like hoes still hit me up on Facebook about him and he swears they in the past and I accept that, but when my past mistake presents itself, I get punished to the highest power, and it's not fair. I understand he's mad, but we could have talked about this and then moved forward together, but the way he's treating me isn't fair. It's making me miserable and depressed. He doesn't talk to me, won't touch me, and barely looks at me. I'm horny, moody, stressed, and depressed. Hell my hair falling out, edges thinning out, and my doctor says I need to eat more. How can I have an appetite when I feel like I want to give up?" I cried having a nervous breakdown. I had been holding all of this on for awhile, and it just spilled over into our conversation. I didn't meant to cry and break down. I only meant to vent to her.

"Don't cry Jasmine, you're going to make me cry," she said tearing up. We had the type of bond that if one of us was hurt, it affected the other.

"I'm trying not to but I can't help it Tommie. My soul hurts like it really hurts deep within," I said, clutching my chest because this shit really was eating me up.

"Oh hell naw, come on because I'm fucking him up got my sister out here mascara running down your face looking like the Crow. No ma'am she said dropping the clothes she had in her hand grabbing the stroller with one hand, and me with the other, and she hit the Sophia from Color Purple walk marching us out of the store and toward the mall exit.

"No Tommie, we not doing this," I half protested. I wanted to confront him, because somebody needed to talk some sense into him. But then I knew how he was, so I half wanted to leave it alone.

"No fuck that, you guys have a child on the way and you will not endanger my nephew, threaten early delivery, or anything because you stressing over this situation. Did you just hear yourself Jasmine? It's affecting your child. Fuck that I'll beat Dom's ass. He has a right to be upset, but this is too damn extreme. Like you said it wasn't like you cheated on him, you fucked Mark when y'all wasn't even together. His ass gone straighten up today," she said going on and on as our security helped us into the car. At this point, I had a headache and didn't even feel like protesting with her. I was trying to mentally prepare myself for the fight that was about to go down at Fly Guys.

***

By the time we got to the store, I had calmed down, and was thinking rationally.

"Tommie, let's not go in there and cause a scene. I promise I'll speak to him when I get home," I said to her, but she just grabbed Royalty and hopped out the car. "We can't be acting like this in front of your child?" I said, still trying to reason with her. I had never seen her this mad, and honestly even my always down to fight ass, was a little scared.

"Fuck that. She good and ain't no muthafuckin' body gone touch her long as her daddy name is Ghost, and he alive and breathing and well." Pulling out my phone, I did a sucker move as I texted Ghost.

Come quick to Fly Guys. Your wife about to go off on Dom and she has Royalty. **Send**

DING!

Tf? What's going on? He immediately texted back

Long story. It's my mess, I told her and she flipped. **Send**.

DING!

I'm on my way, tell her take my damn child and go the fuck home. He said.

I told her and she said ain't nobody gone touch her child as long as her daddy named Ghost and he alive and well. **Send**.

DING!

She called me Ghost? He said.

Yep. Send.

DING!

I'm doing 100 on the highway. She pissed. She might fuck around and beat all our asses, lol. I'm like five minutes away though I'll be pulling up soon. I was headed up there anyway. he said. Putting my way away, I walked into the store to see Julius holding a crying Royalty, and Tommie beating a chick down that I had words with before, involving Dom. I watched as he tried pulling Tommie off her, but she had a tight grip on the girl's hair and won't let go. I wish like hell I wasn't big and pregnant. Shit I could barely see my feet, so I know I wouldn't make shit shake jumping in. Tommie was working that hoe good though.

"Bitch!" *WHAP!* "You!" *WHAP* "got" *WHAP* "my" *WHAP* "sister" *WHAP WHAP* "fucked all the way up!" **WHAP** Tommie yelled, talking to the girl as she whooped her ass.

"Get this crazy ass bitch off of me," the girl screamed as they fell into a clothing rack. Grabbing a crying Royalty from Julius, I said,

"What the hell going on? What she did?"

"The hoe was pushing up on Dominic, and tried popping slick with Tommie trying to show out in front of her friends. The same friends that's watching her get her ass beat," he said pointing towards two females that I just noticed.

"Damn that's tough," I said shaking my head because them hoes were nowhere near the fight. They were literally a good distance away.

"That's what them fake, bougie bitches get. Came in here with them cheap ass two seasons ago, purses popping shit talking about some we look cheap and classless. Chile she tried it with them there no place like home shoes on, fish bye," he said before he flipped his weave over his shoulders and walked back towards the cash register. I wasn't even in the car that long to have missed all of this.

CHAPTER 15

THIS IS NOT HOW I SAW MY DAY GOING

DOM

"So this what we doing now? Like is this really what I have to do to get your attention?" Morgan asked me as she walked into Fly Guys. A nigga really ain't have time for this bullshit, I had enough on my plate. Walking around the counter, I walked up on them.

"We have nothing to talk about. I thought I made that very clear the last time, therefore you shouldn't be trying to get my attention Morgan," I said.

"Harpo, who dis woman?" Julius's crazy ass said.

"Oh trust me, as much as I sat on his face, he knows exactly who I am," she said as the girls behind her started laughing. I had to shake my head and laugh to keep from killing this hoe. She really tried me on the absolute wrong fucking day. It's funny how people's real colors come out when you stop fucking with them.

"Why you up here tryna play yourself, ma? This is not even you though, so what type of shit you on? This is my place of business. I'ma ask you one time to leave before I embarrass you in front of these birds you showing out for," I said.

"Bird? Who you calling bird you lame ass nigga," one of her friends spoke up and said. Just when I was trying to change, bitches wanted to bring the old me out like I won't bat one of their asses in the mouth. I ain't Ghost with that I don't hit females bullshit. Only females off limits was my girl, my brother's girl, and my T-lady. The rest of these hoes can catch a left hook. Like Gates said you duck that one this right bitch won't miss you.

"Again, I'll ask you ladies to leave before y'all are tossed out," I said trying to remain calm. The only thing I was grateful for, was the fact that rush hour was over, so the store was currently empty.

"Please, this cheap ass classless store, I've been put out of way better. Just last week I was upset my food was poorly cooked, and wind up getting put out of Denny's," the other chick said.

"You sure do know how to pick them. I told you you like those busted hoes boss," Julius said.

"Who you calling busted, you he-bitch?" Morgan said.

"That's cute. You tried real hard with that one didn't you? See I don't fight with you hoes, but a queen like me will step down off my throne for a second and read you hoes. With the back of your neck looking like a star crunch. Y'all walked in this bitch matching, looking like a bootleg TLC. If you don't get your don't go chasing waterfalls looking ass on. Bitch you sweating this man, meanwhile your friend to your left leave out crying out to God to let it rain. Shit so fucking dry it's a shame. Over here looking like all my life I had to fight. At least when y'all come somewhere and cause a scene, be on point. You better get in your car, drive off, make a left, and let Siri direct you not to ever come for a queen again," he said as Synthia gave him a high five.

"What you cheering for bitch? You must have had his dick down your throat as well?" Morgan said still refusing to let it go and leave.

"Umm no, I leave that to dirty hoes like you," Synthia said with her nose turned up like the idea of giving head was repulsive. Whelp, I finally figured out why she was single.

"Definitely looking like a dirt dirt," Julius said laughing which caused me to laugh as well. Walking closer to me, she boldly reached out and grabbed my dick.

"Oh I'm dirty Dominic?" She said?

"Hell yeah you dirty, and I advise your dirty ass to back the fuck up." somebody shouted. Turning around, I saw Tommie standing there with her hands on her hips, and a mug on her face. Damn how the fuck did I find myself in this situation?

"And who you supposed to be?" Morgan asked.

"Somebody you don't want to fuck with bitch," Tommie said.

"Aye it ain't what it look like," I said.

"I don't give a fuck what it look like. Instead of you seeing about my fucking sister that's stressed out and pregnant with your fucking child, you out here letting bitches grab your dick?" Tommie yelled.

"Sister? Pregnant? Oh yeah the dark skin hoe from the dressing room. Oh sis stressing? Tell her she ain't got to stress over the dick. Like SZA said, I'll just keep him satisfied every weekend," Morgan said while her minions started laughing. Shit I didn't know Tommie had it in her, and majority of the time I didn't even take her ass seriously, but she shocked the fuck out of a nigga when she opened her mouth and said.

"Funny thing about them lyrics bitch, see Tuesday Wednesday, Thursday Friday, try that shit and I will beat your ass every weekend," Tommie said.

"Please little girl, I haven't always been classy. I'm from the boogie down Bronx, I been about that life, don't let this cute face fool you," Morgan said. I stepped in between them because although Tommie talked a good game, shit first time I saw her, her ass was sporting a black eye. Meanwhile, Morgan look like she'll square up with a nigga. If this was Jas, I wouldn't have to worry, but ion think Ghost told his chick how to boss yet. I ain't got time to be hearing that fool's mouth cause she got beat up in my shit. Nigga be all in his feelings about Tommie's ass.

"Bitch and I'm from Bankhead so what you tryna do?" Tommie said.

"Like I said, I'll take the weekends," Morgan said laughing in Tommie's face. Shit happened to fast even though I was standing right there, I still can't run that shit back to you. Like a nigga blinked and Tommie flew into her ass throwing nothing but haymakers. *Shit my nigga done taught his bitch how to fight*, I thought to myself as I sat there for a second in amazement how she was beating Morgan's ass. Looking up, I expected the hoes she was with to at least jump on Tommie's back or some shit. Man I looked around, and them hoes was halfway on the other side of the damn store. Talking to her as she was beating Morgan's hair, I tried my best to pry Tommie's damn fingers out of her hair. She had a strong ass grip on her shit, and wasn't letting up. I heard Jasmine talking to Julius.

"Take Royalty and go to the car," I yelled at her. She didn't need to be on her feet.

"I'm not going no fucking where until somebody tell me what's going on. What the hell my sister fighting for? Who are these bum ass hoes?" She yelled. By this time, Morgan's friends had finally decided to walk their scary us closer to the fight.

"Who you calling a bum? You fat bitch," The ugly one with the fucked up weave said. I knew she had officially fucked up because if there's one insecurity Jasmine had, it was her weight.

"Dominic you better get this bitch, I'll come out my shoes on this hoe," Jasmine said.

"Come up out them bitches then," the ugly bitch said dropping her bag.

"Naw bitch, you better pick that shit up, take your fucking friends and get the fuck out of here. That's your best bet, because if you think you hitting my baby momma that's pregnant with my fucking seed, I can promise you on your head they won't find your fucking body. You better ask Morgan how a nigga get down," I barked as I finally managed to pull Tommie off Morgan.

"Fuck you Dom with that little ass dick, you can't even hit my damn Gspot. I'm glad I met a real man like Kenneth who know exactly what to do with this pussy," Morgan said.

"Yeah he know what to do with it alright, put it on a corner," I shot back because the nigga thought he was a pimp.

"Nigga, fuck your ugly ass," the friend said.

"Bitch if you don't get your matchbox looking ass on," I said.

"This hoe want me to beat her ass. Ya friend already took an ass whopping from my sister, shit we got more to give out. This a two for one special hoe, what's up?" Jasmine said.

"Let her ass think she fucking hitting you, matter of fact, let me the fuck go so I can beat this hoe up," Tommie said.

"Bitch. fuck you. You need to be worrying about that ugly ass baby and not me," the friend said. Struggling with all of her might to break free from me, Tommie begin screaming and kicking.

"Let me the fuck go! Dom, let me the fuck gooooo!"

"Get y'all ugly ass the fuck out of here before I let her ass go," I yelled.

"Chill Riri, don't even trip, we gon' get our shake back. This hoe had to sneak me, but it definitely ain't over, I'll be back," Morgan yelled as her and her friends all but ran out the damn store when I said I was letting Tommie go.

"And I'll be waiting," Tommie yelled after them breathing heavily, hair widely over her head. Turning to me, her ass swung wildly and caught my ass with a good one as she fought to break free from the grip I had on her arm preventing her from running after them.

"Calm your ass down girl," I said to her.

"Let her go," I heard Ghost bark from behind me.

"Man, where the fuck you was a few minutes ago though?" I said.

"Naw the real question is why the fuck you ain't got this shit under control?" he said snatching Tommie's ass up like it was nothing. "Didn't I say calm your muthafuckin' ass down girl? Make me clown up in this bitch Tommie. Quit trying a real nigga," he said to her.

"Fuck you Ghost. You letting that bitch ass nigga dog my fucking sister out like she some raggedy basic bitch or some shit. Y'all niggas ain't shit. We give and we give, and all y'all do is take and take. To hell with you too, because you prolly knew he was out here wildin' and shit since you don't get in grown folks business. Let me find out one of these ugly ass hoes was here for you," she said still struggling to get loose.

"Aye, get ya girl bruh. A nigga ain't gon' be another bitch," I said raising my voice. I don't know who the fuck she took me for.

"Get that base out ya fucking voice when you talking about my wife nigga," he said to me.

"Shit just let her fucking know," I said. Fuck he thought this was. Nigga don't back down from no fucking body. Brother or not, I'd put his cripple ass down.

"Naw, he don't have to let me know shit," Tommie said trying to square up like she wanted to do something. I had to laugh it off and take two steps backwards, pull my pants up and gather myself together before I rocked off on her ass. I don't know what the fuck that nigga Ghost dealt with, but Jasmine knew her place. She would have never tried me or another man like this in public. Shit that's why her ass was quiet this whole time. Ghost let Tommie's ass get away with murder. A few minutes passed with me and Ghost having an intense stare down before we burst out laughing and dapped each other up.

"I thought y'all was about to start gang banging in here. I was surely going to remind Dominic that that most definitely wasn't in a queen's job description, so I was gone require a raise," Julius said. Without warning, Tommie lunged at me.

"Didn't I say calm your ass the fuck down? You a fucking mother, act like one. Go get my damn child and take your ass home," he said.

"Ima leave when I get ready," she said before Ghost grabbed her to him putting her arms behind her back.

"What the fuck you doing Ghost, get off her like that, she's pregnant," Jasmine yelled.

"Pregnant?" Ghost said and from the look on his face, this was news he didn't know. Turning to look at Jasmine, she had an 'I just fucked up look' on her face.

"Y'all round here talking about us keeping secrets and shit, but look at y'all."

"Don't make this about us because that doesn't change the fact you treating me like a piece of shit, got me stressed out losing weight instead of gaining more weight," she said.

"Well if you losing weight, you should be thanking me since you be complaining anyway about being big," I said jokingly, but apparently she didn't take it that way as tears welled up in her eyes.

"My baby is being put at risk because I'm stressed depressed and being taken through hell all for some shit that happened before we got back together. Shit, your past always getting thrown in my face. I understand that's somebody you used to deal with, but I don't get the same understanding. Hell and used to might not be the right choice of words since she up here wildin' like that, you must be giving her something to act an ass for. If you don't want me fine, I'm done trying. I have a son I have to live for, I'm over your shit. Tommie. I'm headed to the car with Royalty," she said walking off.

"I can explain," Tommie said to Ghost.

"Save it," Ghost said dapping me up and leaving.

"This is your fault," Tommie said to me mugging me as she walked off.

"You need to be mad at your damn self for not telling that man," I said.

"His ass gone have a damn school bus full of them shits after awhile," I said to myself laughing as I started cleaning up the mess they made. Ghost sure was going to need to pay for his crazy ass baby momma fucking shit up. I had underestimated sis, and I like this new her. Yeah I was talking shit to her, but that's just me. You gotta have tough skin in this game, and she definitely handled herself like a boss. Shit she beat the breaks off Morgan's ass, I damn near felt bad for the kid. After the day I had, I was taking my ass home to my own spot, getting in my own bed and crashing. I'd deal with Jasmine tomorrow after she cooled down.

***

Waking up late into the next day, I felt refreshed and relaxed. Yesterday was so damn crazy, I still was tripping off that shit. Turning my phone off, I decided to just kick back at home all day today for once. Watch some of them ratchet tv shows Jasmine liked, and just chilling and catching up on some damn much needed rest. I just didn't feel like dealing with all the shit today. Felt like the weight of the world was beating down on me like a blazing hot fire. Jasmine was supposed to be my calm when shit got rough in these streets, but she couldn't even be that for me right now. Like if I was saving everybody asses and making sure everyone was okay, but who was gonna save me?

Flipping the channel I noticed Love and HipHop New York was on. All this shit ass fake and Mona really needed her ass whooped for tryna play New York like that. I remember the first time Jasmine made me watch this bullshit with her, I was pissed off. Shit full of clown ass washed up ass niggas and artist. Nobody from New York really fucked with nobody like that but Remy, and she barely got a pass. Like where Mona held these auditions at though? She don't even show the true real New York when the cameras be rolling. Shit, they know better than to put a nigga like me on that bitch, I'll make them ratings shoot through the roof though that's for sure. After a few minutes of watching the bullshit, I turned the channel because it wasn't the same without Jasmine's loud ass commentary all throughout the movie. Not long after that, a nigga was knocked out. When I woke back up and looked at the clock, it was a little after six pm. Powering my phone back on, message after message begin flooding my phone.

"Damn nigga can't take a few hours to himself with folks freaking out," I said.

RING RING

Looking down, I noticed an unknown number was calling me.

"What's up nigga?" I asked him.

"What ugly ass hoe you been laid up with that you couldn't answer your phone?" He asked me.

"Shit, maybe ya momma nigga," I said laughing until I noticed he wasn't laughing back. "What's up?" I asked me.

"Man, I can't believe Tommie's ass is pregnant," he said sounding excited as hell.

"Nigga yo ass supposed to be mad they ain't tell you. Your soft ass probably went home like bae it's okay" I said laughing at him.

"Nigga fuck you, just because your beefing with your chick, don't mean I gotta beef with mine. Just for that, I'm not telling you Jas had the locks changed on your stupid ass this morning," he said hanging up the phone. Jumping up, I threw on some clothes and all but flew out the door to Jas' crib. Sure enough after several attempts to get my key to work, it had become apparent that the damn locks had been changed. Ringing the doorbell until she answered the door, she took one look at me and closed that bitch right back. Pulling out my phone, I called her stupid ass, but her petty ass had changed her number that fucking fast.

"This how we ended up in the predicament we was in last time, ol stubborn ass woman. Stop being fucking childish and talk this out with me because I promise on my fucking seed you carrying if I leave, we done. I'm not doing this back and forth shit, we can just co-parent," I shouted. After waiting about ten minutes, I turned to leave until I heard the locks click.

"In order to co-parent, the child would need to be yours," she said. Before I could make sense of what I was doing, a nigga had pulled my gun out quick as fuck on her ass.

"I'll kill you and that fuck nigga and raise my son my damn self before I let another nigga do it, stop playing with me Jas," I said. Catching myself, I put my gun away just as her ass kicked me dead in the balls. Once I doubled over, she real life pulled some mace out from behind her back that I just noticed was there. Before I could threaten to fuck her up if she maced me, her crazy ass damn near emptied the entire bottle on my ass. Just when I thought the shit was over and she had gotten her point across, this short ass pregnant demon went to mixing on a nigga. No white girl licks either, but her little ass really was hitting my ass hard as hell. Burning eyes and all, I managed to grab her up and back us into the house because one I didn't want the neighbors to see me getting my ass beat and think shit was sweet. Hell if they ever tried their luck, she'd have to move, because I would empty this whole fucking block out. I also didn't want my baby momma out here wilding like that. Listening to her yell out how I had made her feel this entire time made me feel real fucked up, so I stood there and took the licks, until she got it all out of her system. I was fucked up for that shit, and didn't even stop to take into consideration how the shit made her feel in all of this. Once she had tired herself out, I went to wash my damn eyes, before I grabbed a bottle and made my way back to where she was. By this time, she was laying on the floor.

"You better not have hurt my son while you done went all Tina Turner What's Love Got To Do With it on a nigga and shit." I said, laughing. She couldn't help but laugh as well as she sat up and took the bottle of water out of my hand. "Real talk though, I'm sorry. I love you, and our son," I said confessing my love putting it all on the table.

RING! RING!

Glancing down at the unavailable number, I started not to answer, but I said fuck it, and went ahead and answered it.

"Yo?" I said.

"Checkmate," they said.

"What?" I said until I heard Jacinta screaming in the background. My eyes grew big as saucers as I ran out the house. I didn't even realize Jas had ran with me until I heard the passenger side door opening.

"Go your ass back in the house Jasmine. You're pregnant," I said in a panicked voice.

"Hell no, I'm going wherever my nigga going. I got your back," she said. Not having time to argue with her hard headed ass, I pulled out the drive way and broke every traffic law to make it to Jackie's crib on the other side of town. When I got there, I barely parked before I was out the car.

"Jackie, Jacinta where y'all at?" I called out to them as I burst into the house. The shit looked like a tornado had hit to how couches were cut up and turned over. Still I walked towards the back. As soon as I opened Jackie's door, I immediately ran to her. Laying in the middle of her flood, bloody, beaten, and barely breathing was Jackie. Rushing over to her, I took my shirt off and covered her as best as I could. Though I didn't have love for her in a sexual relationship way, I would always love her because she was my first everything. First love, first heartbreak, first baby momma, and first almost wife.

"Dom," she said coughing up blood.

"Shhh, don't speak," I said.

"I wouldn't let him take my baby. I tried. I told him over my dead body. Please," she said coughing up more blood. "Please get my baby back Dominic. I know I haven't always done right, but I love my baby, please don't let him hurt my baby. Promise me. Promise me you'll get her back and keep her." She said.

"Dom move baby, let me help her," I heard Jasmine say, but I refused to let Jackie go as tears rolled down my face.

"Dom I'm a doctor, let me help her," Jasmine screamed. At this point she was emotional and crying as well. We both knew she was beyond help. Her face was almost caved in, she was beaten that badly.

"I put this on my life, I'ma get her back ma, or die trying. I'll be damned if anything ever happens to her as long as I got breath in my body. I promise you that." I said rocking her slowly as I heard sirens getting closer. Reaching up and grabbing my chin, she smiled a weak smile and I felt her body take its last breath.

CHAPTER 16
I CAN'T JUST SIT BACK AND DO NOTHING….

TOMMIE

I was excited about my doctor's appointment today not because I got to see my munchkin, but because I got to see Landon. Ever since Jacinta was kidnapped and Jackie was killed, Landon hasn't been home. I understand he's not only trying to be there for his friend, but find whoever was behind this. I just wish he could find a balance so that I didn't have to go without him and get the short end of the stick. I didn't know if that was selfish or not, so I didn't mention it to him because I had just got my ass out the dog house. Not only did he barely talk to me after he found out I kept being pregnant a secret, but he cut me off from sex knowing how horny I get when I'm pregnant. Then to take petty to a new level, he found all of my sex toys and took the batteries out of them. I straightened up quick as hell. I was almost ready to get on my hands and knees and beg but after he left Dom at the hospital, he came home fucked me into the middle of next year, then just held me tightly as his body shook uncontrollably. I know Jackie's death shook him up for a lot of different reasons. That was the last time I really got to be that close to him. He said he wasn't resting until this person or person was caught. They had been out in the streets making so much noise, that the police came by the shop with a search warrant and to arrest Landon for Henry's death. With them burning down Kenneth's whore house, killing literally every one of his girls, and wrecking all types of havoc, I'm sure he slipped up somewhere giving the cops some ammo to charge him. Whereas before they didn't have a leg to stand on, it seemed like they had found one. Worse of all, Kenneth's ass had disappeared off the face of the earth. Each girl they tortured before killing all said the same thing, they didn't know where he was, and he didn't tell them. They supposed to be flying to Atlanta next week sometime to see what the streets were saying that way.

"Tommie Knowles," the nurse said calling my name. I took my time getting up as I glanced around once more to see if I spotted Landon. When I didn't see him, I walked slowly to the back. My feelings were beyond hurt at this point. Once the nurse had weighted me, and checked my pressure, I made myself comfortable on the bed as I awaited the doctor, I laid back on the bed with my eyes closed. Feeling wet lips on mine, my eyes popped open quickly in alarm only to see Landon over me. Kissing my man back passionately, I broke the kiss and sat up.

"You almost missed it," I said folding my arms over my chest.

"Never," he said handing my roses. "I know you think I haven't been around, but really I'm with you everyday all day," he said.

"Huh?"

"I'm just not with you visibly. It's someone that's watching us. If I'm not seen with you, they might slip up and try their luck at getting to you. I am in the shadows lurking. By the way, cut that shit you be doing with Curtis out for real. Nigga almost shot my own damn shop up yesterday because y'all asses wanted to try me like I got all my damn screws," he said.

"I won't ever talk to him again," I quickly said not because I was scared he'd shoot the store up. I was positive his ass would do that, I just didn't want to spend the little time I had with him right now arguing. I would agree to anything at this point.

"Knock knock," the doctor said as she came into the room. "How are we doing this afternoon, mommy?" She said. Looking up at Landon, I said,

"Much better."

"Well that's definitely what we like to hear. Let's take a look at your peanut and see if everything is going okay with him." She said. I had found out two visits ago that I was having a son, and couldn't be more happier about it. Hell I was more excited than Landon because that meant this was my last rodeo with this. Hell, now he has his son and daughter. It's a wrap.

"So this is our second bundle of joy correct?" The doctor said.

"Yes," I said.

"Do we plan on having anymore?" She asked as she begin applying the gel.

"No."

"Yes," Landon and I answered at the same time.

"Uh uh mommy, looks like daddy didn't inform you of that one," she said.

"Yes? Really Landon? You have a daughter, and now a son. What else you need?"

"I want at least three more," he said causing me to look at me as if he had sprouted two heads. I don't know what the hell he been smoking, but he surely had been fucked up if he thought I was pushing three more kids out.

***

"I'm on my way," I told Jasmine as I weaved in and out of traffic rushing to the hospital. Her water had broken finally, and she was in labor. I was so ready for her grouchy ass to have this baby, it wasn't even funny. Landon had called me and told me that he and Dom should be touching down any minute now, and they were coming straight to the hospital. They had barely been gone a day, and now that Jas was having the baby, I doubt they'd go bac. That was good news for me. I knew for a fact Dominic wouldn't leave her and the baby.

"This hurts so freaking bad Tommie, I'm sorry for even laughing at you or thinking you was exaggerating. They said I'm too far along for an epidural," she cried. "Fuck, I'm not gone make it much longer, I'm hurting too badly, I'm dying Tommie. I think I see the light, I'm going up to heaven," her dramatic said, and I thought I was dramatic. Whipping my truck into the first parking space I saw, I got out and ran inside.

"I'm here now, I'll be up in a second." I said disconnecting the all as I got her room number before I rushed to labor and delivery. Stepping off the elevator and into the waiting room, I immediately got a headache as I seen Dr. Mark sitting there with his slacks and button down on looking every bit like a square ass dude. I mean don't get me wrong, it's nothing wrong with the clean cut look. Landon likes to switch it up and throw on a tailored suit, or slacks and a button down as well. But even dressed up, he still had the aura about him that screamed he was *that* nigga.

"Before you say anything, that could be my baby in there, and I'm not leaving. I don't want any drama. Hell, I'm not desperate, nor broke. I make just as much legal money as her thug boyfriend, and could without a doubt have any girl I wanted. I'm not here for her, just the baby," he said. I almost asked how he knew she was in labor, but remember he was a prestigious black doctor, and knew a lot of fellow doctors in every state like Jasmine did. So I'm sure he had them put him on standby for when she had her baby.

"My sister told me she did a prenatal paternity test," I said.

"Did she ever tell you the results?" He asked me as I shook my head.

"Shit, me either. That's why I'm here," he said. Maybe he really is concerned only about the child. Lord, pleasedon't let him die today, I thought as my phone begin to ring.

"Hello?"

"Ghost, tell Tommie she better tell Jasmine to squeeze her legs tightly together and keep his lil' ass in there until we make it. She know how to squeeze, tell her just like she be squeezing this dick," I heard Dom yelling through the phone.

"Nigga I'm not about to tell my girl no bullshit like that. She don't give a fuck how nobody squeezing shit." Landon said.

"Hello?" He said.

"Yes I'm here, Landon." I said.

"Tell Jasmine we on the way and disregard that extra shit that nigga taking about, and I wish you would repeat some dumb shit like that." This crazy fool said really getting mad like it was my idea to say the shit. I swear he could really get a check. There has to be a real life disorder that he has.

"Whatever, I'll tell her. Heads up, Mark here," I said quickly hanging up because that's one conversation I didn't want to hear. I'm not sure if it was because he was at the hospital and his son was about to be born, or if Landon had had a talk with him, but Dom didn't say anything to Mark as he rushed off the elevator and into her room just as I was coming out of the room.

"Finally y'all made it." I said to Landon as he went to get suited up. I felt slightly bad for Mark that he didn't get to come into the room just in case it was his child. I mean I know he had to have hopped on a flight as soon as he got the call, so that should have counted for something. That would really push Dom over the edge though, so maybe it was a good idea for him to just stay where he was.

At 10:15pm on May 2, 2017, Dominic Reynolds Jr made his way into the world screaming his head off. One look at him, and you could tell he was the spitting image of his father. Jr looked so much like Dom, you would think he pushed his ass out himself. He was so handsome, and chubby with a head full of hair. I couldn't wait to have my son, and was excited about what he would look like. Hopefully he wouldn't have Landon's big ass head.

***

"You're late," I said to Samantha as I looked at my watch as she came walking in.

"Oh my bad, she said like it wasn't really a big deal. I let a lot slide around here because I wasn't tryna be too strict, but she was over an hour late. I'm pretty sure she would have called Landon and let me know ahead of time if she was running late, and I demanded the same respect.

"Your bad? Cool when you clock in, make sure you clock right back out and go home." I said.

"What? I need my hours. You can't do that shit," she said.

"Oh my bad," I said taking a sip of my Starbucks as I walked into Landons office that I was slowly making into my own. A few minutes later, I heard a knock at the door.

"Come in," I said as Samantha walked inside of my office and closed the door.

"I'm too pregnant to be giving out ass whoopings, but I can promise you I'll reach my gun before you reach me," I said, calmly taking another sip from my caramel frappuccino.

"I'm not on that tip. Look, I'm sorry for my behavior, and I was late because my weak ass baby daddy was supposed to get my baby for me, but at the last minute, he called talking about something came up. I never ask him for anything, but my babysitter canceled, and he was my only other option. It's hard enough being a single parent, and sole provider for her, least he can do is watch her. I was late running around trying to find someone to watch her which I found a day care but they high, and I just gave them my last $100. I'm barely making ends meet, the daycare was non-refundable today, and I really need my job," she said fighting back tears. I still didn't like her ass, but I wasn't heartless. I was a mother as well, so I knew it could be difficult. I mean granted I had a good man, and a nanny, so I didn't know her exact struggle, but I knew it was still hard.

"Listen, everyone has troubles in life, that's no excuse to not do your job, if anything it should have you go harder knowing she'll suffer if you fuck up. You can stay on the clock, but I'm writing you up, I'll have it ready to sign later on. I'll clock you in from the time you were originally scheduled to be here," I said to her. Thanking me, she walked one of the office. Logging onto his computer, I began looking for something that would tell me how to even write her up, because I had never done that before, when I stumbled upon his Facebook account that was saved as a thumbnail on his computer. *Just keep strolling,* I pep talked myself clicking off the page, until a little red devil appeared on my shoulder. The devil was me with a red dress on, red stripper thigh high boots, with red lipstick. Devil Tommie said,

"Bitch you better stop and go look through his messenger to see what hoes be talking to him, and who he responding to." That's exactly what I did and I pulled his account back up, clicking o inbox messages. The thirst was real as I scrolled by nude pics, long thirst trap messages, and bitches trying to get his attention. None of these messages were opened which was a relief and made me feel all bubbly inside. One in particular stood out from the rest. It started by saying this is urgent in all caps. Immediately clicking on the message, I read it twice before I looked to see when it was sent, and who sent it. Clicking on the profile, I saw that it was deleted. The inbox basically said that Amber was responsible for having guys shoot up Fly Guys, and it detailed a plan that Kennth, Amber and Kelina had to Kidnap Royalty for ransom money. It would make sense that two made bitter bitches would link up. But see where they fucked up at was playing with my child. Grabbing my purse and keys,I let my team know I was leaving as I rushed home to tell my man the good news. The inbox also said where they met at, and where they was ducked off at. Damn Landon had the answers to all his problems this entire time, he just never opened his messenger. The real question now was, who sent it?

CHAPTER 17

NIGGAS FUCKED ADOUND AND LET ME SHAKE BACK....

RODNEY

"Daddy I'm hungry," Karter said as he came jumped on my bed with me. I know y'all didn't think I wouldn't see my baby? Believe it or not, I loved the fuck out this lil' nigga. I mean I know I had a funny way of showing it on account I rarely fucked with him when he was a secret, but ever since I accepted the fact that he was my seed, it's been all about him. Since Chelsea and Amber tight, Chelsea would get Karter and bring him to me. She'd even keep him a few nights. His deadbeat ass mammy didn't give a fuck one way or the other anyway. When I made my escape, in a few days, I was taking my little man with me. We needed a fresh start, and his mammy would be dead soon anyway, if everything went as planned. Chelsea had already heard back from Ghost, since I told her to leave a burner number. Things were moving forward as planned, so shit who else would my son after that evil bitch Amber got what was coming to her? I know for a fact that nigga was killing her ass, and he most definitely would figure out Chelsea was working with her.

"Karter, get off that bed with your shoes still on."
My ma dukes said. I also broke down and contacted her, and
instead of cursing me out like I thought she would, she
actually was happy as hell to hear from a nigga. I couldn't
stand to see her hurting and grieving for me and I wasn't
dead, the shit was eating me up, besides a nigga caught a
fucking infection, and who better to take care of me than my
momma? No matter how she felt about me, my momma
wouldn't turn her back on me. It killed me to bring her into
this messy situation though, but if I don't know anything
else, I know Ghost wouldn't allow any harm to come to her.
Shit his ass probably loved her more than I did. So I didn't
have to worry about her paying for my mistakes. Besides, she
didn't even know Ghost shot me, she thinks some fools
robbed and shot me. Last but not least, just as I had hopped,
my nigga Monsta had found his way to the spot. I knew if he
was alive, he'd come here. Shit instead of letting them niggas
hang themselves, he had to get in on the action by cutting
that nigga Dom's baby momma up. That nigga lived for shit
like that with his throwed off ass. I was taking all them and
dipping out. I had moved more than enough money to get out
of town, and start over. Once I was safely settled, I'd just
take the rest of my shit not giving a fuck if they noticed or
not.

"Oay granny, and I'm hungry," Karter said. Getting up from the bed, I walked into the kitchen behind my momma, to see what we had to cook. Since she's been here, it felt like my health improved literally overnight. I felt better, I was getting my weight back up, and healing up nicely.

"When are we leaving?" She asked me.

"Next week," I said to her, still happy she agreed to come with me.

"I think we should leave tonight, I don't like the idea of you being here a minute longer. Something is bothering my spirits, and I don't know what it is, but we need to leave tonight," she said. I just stared at her intensely for awhile before I said,

"Okay have everything packed up by 9. Ima have Monsta make a few calls for me to get us on a flight out tonight," I said to her causing her to smile. Making her happy made me happy, if she wanted to leave tonight we would. Besides, the only reason I was staying was to see this shit play out, but now that I think about it, having front row seats had some many different outcomes that didn't end in my favor, that's I'd settle for seeing R.I.P stats on facebook.

***

"Daddy, look at the sky, it's pretty," Karter said pointing out the window from our first class seats.

"He's so adorable," a pretty, light skinned chick said. Judging by her attire, you could tell she was a business woman.

"Yeah, he's an adorable handful," I said.

"Aww well at least you have him and giving is mom a break, theirs lots of men who don't do that," she said. I like what she did there. In a classy way, checked to see if a nigga was still with my baby's mom or not.

"Yeah I'm a single parent, so I have no choice but to have him all the time," I said flashing her my award-winning smile. This new life thing was starting off with a bang. I had already secured a new woman, and my little nigga would have a new momma. I would settle down for now, but I damn sure was coming back with a vengeance for everything that was taken from me.

CHAPTER 18
CHECKMATE....

GHOST

"So why now? What made you come back to find me now?" I asked Betty as we sat in my living room talking. I had gotten the closure I needed from my foul ass aunt, and now I needed this talk with the lady who gave birth to me. So when she showed up on my doorstep, I couldn't turn her away.

"Because I wanted to make amends with my boys, I owed you guys that much. A few years ago, I was diagnosed with breast cancer," she said and I immediately felt a piercing feeling in my chest like I was looking my mother all over again.

"Boys? A nigga got a brother? Wait, you dying?" I said.

"Dang Landon hush, so I can finish." She told me. Laughing, I didn't say anything else as she continued.

"I felt like I was going to die as I was brought into the hospital suffering from a drug overdose. Instead of me taking my medicine for the cancer, I had been selling the pills in exchange for drugs. It made my cancer flare up really badly. I was in the hospital for about two months because the doctor refused to release me. She said I was a danger to myself, and the rate I was doing, I would be dead before the week was out. I underwent surgery after surgery, pill after pill, but nothing seemed to be working. The cancer had turned aggressive, and was attacking my body with a vengeance. I figured this was my karma for abandoning both of my kids. After I was forced to leave you, I was so bad on drugs, that I was doing things I'm not proud of just to get more. That resulted in me having your baby brother, Kameron. I tried really hard to do right by him since I was given a second chance at motherhood, but that drug demon was on my back, and I couldn't beat it alone, so I once again lost another child. The state took him from me. So there I was on my death bed hooked up to all kinds of machines, with a fever that wouldn't break, and a pain in my heart that I couldn't shake. I was hurting because as I looked around me, I didn't see anyone. The nurses asked me daily if I had someone to call, someone to come be with me, and I had no one. I didn't want to die alone, I didn't want to die without seeing my kids again. I cried out to God that day, and told him that if he allowed me to live a little while longer, I would make sure I got clean, finished school because before your aunts got me on drugs, I wanted to be a nurse. So I made a promise that I would finish school no matter how long it look, and do right by my kids. I wanted to find each of you, and try and make amends before I died. I didn't die that day, and the day I was well enough to go home, I checked myself into a drug rehabilitation center. Once I got out, I enrolled back in school, graduated, and set out on my search to find my babies. I found Kameron in Dallas since I was around that area when I had him. I would say you have to talk to him, but because you not any better," she said laughing.

"Hey what's that supposed to mean? The lifestyle I live doesn't mean I can't hit my dude with some wisdom. Shit, a nigga got a little brother. What is he like? Bad as hell? Fighting and shit?" I said firing off question after question. I envisioned a bad ass misguided teenager out here pushing nickel bags and thinking he hard. Big brother could take him under my wing, and mold him into a beast. The thought of connecting with him brought a new a feeling that I couldn't even explain. I thought I would be upset, or reject Betty, but I surprised the hell out of myself how drawn I was to her. They say no matter how old you are, a child will always know their mother, and I've been getting maternal vibes from her since I first met her. Laughing, she said,

"I'm not sure what type of kid brother Kameron is, but he is crazy as hell just like you. He calls himself Killa, and runs with an even crazier guy named Danger," she said. Putting my hand on my chin, I had to think long and hard because that name sounded familiar. Then like a lightbulb going off in my head, I said,

"Shit I know fucking Danger's ass. We did business once. I met him through Midos one time. I vaguely remember Killa though," I said thinking back to that day when we all linked up. I remember a big nigga with a beard standing off to the side mugging and Dom made a crack about he must be the watch dog. Danger said that was his right hand Killa, and his ass cool he always looking mean. So that was a nigga little big brother. I made a mental note to make my way to Dallas in the near future so I could link with them. Betty went to open her mouth, but Tommie came running through the door.

"Aye bae, check it out. A nigga gotta baby brother," I said with pride in my voice. I felt like I had lost a brother when I got at Rodney, but now things were looking up. Breathing heavily, she struggled to catch her breath as she said something about Facebook.

"What?" I asked her?

"Look at your Facebook messenger," she said still breathing heavily.

"Facebook messenger? Why? And damn did you run all the way here?" I said looking at her in confusion.

"Just look Ghost. Damn," She said.

"Ghost huh?" I said pulling my phone out and clicking on messenger app. The first thing I saw was a picture from some hoe bent over flashing her pussy from the back. *Damn they wilding like this on my shit? I never even seen these joints. Okay, let me not look too hard while Tommie ass standing over a nigga and shit. Okay, just plead the fifth nigga or your ass definitely not getting no pussy tonight.*

"Say bruh a nigga don't know shit about any of this. None of these messages even open so I'm saying what you running over here for damn near about to kill your self to get me to look at my inbox full of hoes that hasn't been opened? You know how I feel about that insecurity shit. Has a nigga ever given you a reason to question your position in my life?" I said getting pissed off now that I think about it. She pregnant with my seed and did all that damn running for this bullshit.

"Shut your stupid ass up and look at this message," she said snatching the phone out of my hand, clicking on a message, then handing it to me. I stared at her intensely for a few moments clenching my jaw as I thought of ways to fuck her up without actually fucking her up. I would never put my hands on her, despite that reckless ass mouth she had. I was most definitely beating her shit out the frame tonight though. She wasn't getting out that bed for at least a few days after I finished murdering her shit. Finally looking down at the message she was showing me, my eyes went from light brown to charcoal black as I read and re read the message.

***

"Why this shit feel like deja vu us stalking out a house and shit? This the same scenario we was just in a couple months back with Rodney's bitch ass. Waiting outside his factory for his dusty ass," I said passing the blunt to Dom.

"Hell yeah. Aye. no lie that shit was fucking epic how that damn factory exploded, and we started popping niggas who ran out. Man we was on some mafia type shit that night. I'm almost mad the nigga Rodney didn't have more fight in him," Dom said.

"Shit I'm not mad, I knew he was a pussy. He wasn't shit without a weapon. I was always fighting his battles for him growing up. Now if he would have ate a few bullets, and still got up or pulled out his gun, then maybe I would have been surprised," I said. "Aye nigga pass me my shit back fuck," I said to him because the nigga was holding my blunt hostage and shit.

"Damn I ain't even hit the shit ol' crying ass nigga. Here," he said passing it back. Looking around at our surroundings, he said,

"This where the tracker pinned at?"

"Naw we just parked at an abandoned house in the heart of the hood because we tryna buy a dub," I said because that was a dumb ass question. Why else would our asses be over here. Shit was so dirty, I wouldn't let my dog live here. I knew some grimy niggas that lived this way though.

"Fuck you shit. I didn't figure a bitch who just came up on fifty million would bring the shit back to this damn rat trap. A nigga could easily kick this shit down and take all that shit. So unless she packing some major heat, she dumb ass hell. Fuck she could have even went to Motel 6," he said. With the help of Matthew, the IP address from the Facebook page that messaged me was traced back to Chelsea's ass. It didn't take a rocket scientist to figure out she had turned on all of their asses. Snitching most definitely wouldn't save her though, she would get it first because snitches get stitches.

"You

re right but this coming from the same chick that used her own damn email address to make a fake page, like the hoe clearly isn't that bright," I said.

DING!

Looking down at my phone, I saw a text that simply read

Found Kenneth, he might dip out soon, here's his location. A smile crept on my face just as another thought came to me. Pulling out my cell phone, I called Tommie.

"Hello? You good, bae?" She asked me in a panicked voice. It took me choking her ass against the wall and fucking her to sleep, to get her to stay her pregnant ass at home. Every since she learned to drive, she swore she was GI Jane or some shit.

"Yeah quit stressing. You gon' upset my damn son and I'll have to fuck you up. Listen, get in touch with your twin cousins for me, the ones in the wedding," I said.

"You didn't have to say the ones in the wedding, because I only have one set of twin cousins," she said matter of factly.

"You knew what the hell I meant, smart ass. Just hit them up and have them to call me," I said as a smile spread across my face at the shit that was to come. This what a nigga had been putting in work with the physical therapist for, this very moment. They done fucked around and let a nigga get back to a one hundred percent, and it was game time now.

"So what's up? You ready to run in this bitch and get shit popping?" Dom asked me.

"Naw, I'ma let the twins put in work. They been asking for months to get down, and this their first assignment," I said just as my phone begin to ring. "We got another fish we need to catch," I said answering the phone for Kenyatta and Kenya.

CHAPTER 19
I SPY A FUCK NIGGA…..

DOM

"Why should I help you after you dogged me out and let that bitch sneak me? Morgan asked me. We had gotten the drop on Kenneth, but I knew he still had Jacinta with him. I needed to get her safely away before we moved in on his ass. I didn't want to start blasting, until I knew she was safe. I made a promise to Jackie, and I had to deliver. Since Morgan and Kenneth were messing around at one point, I knew he'd trust her to come over.

"I told you you got your ass beat by sis for talking shit. I'm with her sister, you thought she was gone let you push up on me and not see about that? I don't know what you want a nigga to do about you getting your ass beat. But, I can pay for you some boxing lessons or something," I said to her truthfully. All that mouth she had, and didn't even pinch Tommie's ass. She fucked her ass up, and she not even a fighter.

"Fuck you Dominic," She spat.

"I'm saying shawty. like Tommie ain't even a fighter, and she gave your ass the business, so those lessons could come in handy," I said shrugging.

"Aye nigga, that's my wife you talking about. My baby got some scrap in her once you push her buttons," Ghost said. Ignoring his ass, I had to bite my tongue and turn on the charm. I just hope Jas didn't find out and kill both our asses. Our relationship was still rocky, and slowly trying to get better, this would set us all the way back.

"Listen ma, you just caught me at a fucked up point in my life where another chick already had my heart. You beautiful and bad as hell, and I kick myself every day for shit even getting to the point it got to. I should have just told you what it was from jump. Don't let our history turn you into a bitter angry person. You bad as hell, and any nigga you run across gone be lucky as hell to wife you up. I'm sorry if I hurt you because that was never my intentions, a nigga just was in love and fighting my feelings," I said hitting her with an award winning smile and I pushed her hair behind her ear. I was half honest, half lying my ass off. I was however in love with Jasmine, and fighting my feelings by messing with Morgan until Jasmine got her shit together. Morgan started tearing up as she said,

"That's all I ever wanted was an apology. I accept it because it was beautiful," she said giving me a hug. Glancing up at Ghost, the nigga was trying so hard to hold his laugh in. Shaking my head, I pulled away from her.

"So you gone help me out bae?" I asked her.

"You know it," she said causing a huge smile to spread across my face.

"Okay, this is what I need you to do," I said, running down the plan to her.

***

BOOM!

Kicking down the door to the apartment Kenneth was staying in, we rushed in as his ass struggled to put his clothes on. He was currently getting head from a crackhead with no teeth in her mouth. While he scrambled to pull his pants up, her ass just sat there naked as the day she was born.

"What the fuck?" he said attempting to dive for his gun, but Ghost shot in that direction, making him rethink that idea.

"Nigga, no you not letting this rotten mouth bitch suck you up? And the bitch cutting up," I said holding my hand over my nose because the odor coming from her should be illegal.

"Damn this bitch is funky as hell. I don't know if that's that's her cat or body smelling like a skunk died, but nigga you wild as hell for letting that bitch anywhere near your dick," Ghost said.

"I need my money," the lady spoke up saying looking zoned out. Looking around, she finally noticed us. Taking in our appearance, I guess she figured she had scored big. "You brought friends. I need this money, so I'm down for whatever," she said crawling towards Ghost, who let off three rounds into her head. Looking at him, he said,

"Fuck you looking at nigga? I wasn't letting that bitch get any closer to me. Stanky ass smelling like death and shit. Fuck all that," he said laughing. Turning my attention back to Kennth, I said,

"All that big boy shit you was doing, and this where you was holed up at? I'm disappointed nigga. How you fucked Jackie up, I just knew you was about to be difficult to take down. Shit, but we catch you slipping with pants down. I was gone make this painful for you, but you not even worth it," I said.

"Fuck all that, Jackie may was strung out on that shit, but she was like family, so I got all the time in the world," Ghost said as he walked over and hit Kenneth in the head with his gun knocking him out. "Come pick this nigga up, and let's get his ass back to the warehouse. It's been a minute since I opened my chamber, but this bitch just earned himself a first class ticket," he said, walking out the apartment and stepping all on the damn crackhead in the process. I could only shake my head because that nigga was officially back, and there was about to be hell to pay.

***

Once we had gotten Kenneth back to the warehouse and inside the soundproof dungeon, that crazy ass nigga Ghost, stripped him down to his boxers, and had his feet and hands tied together and stretched out as if he were on a cross. Hearing commotion coming from the adjoining room, we both pulled our guns out and walked over to the door. Pushing it open, there in the middle of the room sat Menace with a bloody and beaten Vivian tied up to a similar bed.

"Damn nigga this where your ass been? And what's going on in here because I'm so confused, I thought Vivian was in the hospital?" Ghost asked.

"Oh this is Vanessa, Vivian's identical twin sister. Vivian, is over there," he said walking over to a chair in the corner that I just noticed, and snatched a bag off of Vivian's head.

"Nigga did you snatch the hoe up out of the hospital?" I asked, because she still had her gown on. If Vanessa was behind everything, then why was Vivian tied up? Shit was getting crazier by the minute.

"You see, when Ghost said he saw my shit, I knew it was no way Vanessa could have gotten my car unless she walked right past the gate and into my house since she looked just like Vivian. The only problem with that is, Vivian had to tell her the layout of the house, and where I kept the keys to the Bentley at," he said. "They may be identical twins, but only Vivian's eye can be scanned to get into that room. So they pulled a switch on my ass. Vanessa was with me out to sea, and Vivian was the one who went to meet the feds. I don't know how I missed the shit until I remembered that night I was fucked up and recalled the sex. Vanessa was acting like that was our first time fucking, and couldn't take the dick, whereas Vivian's used to it.

"No, she set me up," Vivian said weakly.

"You know I don't like Vivian's ass, but I don't think she was behind all this. Too much shit done came to the light," Ghost said, and I had to agree.

"I was leaving her, and had cut her out of my will," Menace said dropping a bomb on all of us. "Them hoes almost pulled off the perfect plan, but I guess Vanessa got greedy and double crossed Vivian, shooting her to eliminate her from the game. Vivian os a lot of things, but she's never harmed me, and my guess is Vanessa wanted me dead. Probably because I would never fuck her in the past. She been jealous of her sister her entire life, and Vivian is desperate for her sister's love, so she never even saw it. She was jealous of everything she had, and would do anything to have her life. Vanessa may have in fact been the mastermind behind all of this, and manipulated Vivian, but she sealed her own fate as soon as she turned snitch," he said emptying a full clip inside of Vivian. *Damn, how was a nigga gone explain this to Jasmine?* I thought.

"I'll tell my daughter in my own way," Menace said as if reading my mind. Going back to where Vanessa was, he picked up a bucket and threw it on top of her head. When I saw big ass cock roaches coming out the bucket, I quickly jumped back.

"Say man what the fuck!" I yelled. "Why you just ain't shot the hoe like you did Vivian?" I asked as the roaches attached a screaming Vanessa.

"Because I loved Vivian," was his only reply before he walked off. Ghost nodded his head like he understood that logic as his equally crazy ass followed behind him.

"If we ever fall out, I'm shooting both of you crazy muthafuckas before y'all even get a chance to try some sick shit like that on my ass," I yelled as I walked off behind them. Walking back into the room past Kenneth who was awake and struggling to free himself, we walked back up the stairs into the main area of the warehouse. I would deal with him in a minute. Torturing wasn't my area of expertise, but for what he did to Jackie, the nigga was most definitely gonna feel me. We had just sat down when two girls dressed alike in blue jean jackets, blue jeans ripped up pants that were hugging the fuck out of their curves just right, and matching J's walked in. Both of their asses were bad as hell. I couldn't look away even if I wanted to.

"What's up, Ghost?" One of the twins spoke up as she popped some bubble gum all loud and ratchet like.

"Kenyatta, Kenya, what's good? Y'all got my package?" Ghost said.

"Aye, who's this?" I asked him.

"This is Kenyatta, and Kenya, Tommie's twin cousins. They been asking to get down, so I gave them the task of getting my bread back, and handling that issue with Chelsea," Ghost said. Looking past them, I didn't see anything, only the duffel bag with the money, and an additional bag.

"Shit they fine and all, but you should have gave them another task, or been more specific. We could have stolen our on shit back, that ain't handling the situation," I said. Looking at each other smiling, the twin holding a smaller back chunked it at me. Catching the bag, I dumped it out on the table, and out rolled Chelsea's head.

"Looks handier to me," they both said in unison.

"Y'all bitches is just as crazy as these muthafuckas," I said jumping up and kicking the head away from me. "Am I the only nigga that still shoots people? Damn y'all got issues," I said.

"Aye, handle that nigga in there. I got one more person to take care of," Ghost said to me as he took half the money out the bag, threw the rest back to the twins, and walked out the room.

CHAPTER 20
TAG, YOU'RE IT

GHOST

"Still can't cook," I said to Kelina as she came inside her kitchen, and cut on the light. I was sitting at her table, trying eat some type of pasta her ass had called herself cooking. That's one thing I had missed about Tommie when I was with Kelina, those homemade meals. This bitch couldn't boil water. And still her ass was dirty as fuck, judging by all the empty food cartons, and bags laying around. It's a wonder her pussy ain't dirty by how she keep her house. A nigga would have never know how down bad she was, because when we were together, my shit stayed clean. Her eyes got real buck when she saw me sitting at her raggedy ass table eating. It's funny how the bitch had all the heart in the world to shoot me, but now her face looked like she had seen a ghost, pun intended.

"Ghost. Wha-at are you doing here?" She stuttered.

"Wha-at do you think I'm doing here?" I asked, mimicking her ass as I pushed my bowl away. "This don't make no damn sense this shit taste so bad. I see why you still got a pot full still. Hell, you might as well just throw the shit away. Putting it in the refrigerator like you gon' eat this nasty shit." Regaining her composure, and trying to save face, she said,

"Somebody like it, now what you want? Why you in my house?" She asked me.

"So that's the game we playing? Acting like you innocent and this just a social visit? Get it off your chest, what's your problem with me? Mad that I left you for Tommie? What? What made you shoot me and mastermind all this shit?" I asked her. Instead of answering me, she started laughing hysterically.

"Why? Why? You want to know why Ghost?" She said, her fingers now twitching.

"This doesn't have anything to do with Tommie's fat ass, this is about you. I hate niggas like you who play daddy to a bitch's kids that's not even yours, but a deadbeat to your own fucking seed," she yelled. If I didn't think the bitch was crazy before, I most definitely knew she was looney now.

"Kids? What the hell you talking about, Kelina?" I said.

"Oh now it's what the hell I'm talking about? So you amnesia now nigga is that it? Okay, bitch let me refresh your memory, follow me," she said walking out the room and I quickly followed her with my gun drawn just in case her was tried some goofy shit that got her popped before I was ready for her ass to die. Walking into the living room, she walked over to a drawer, pulled a book out, and threw it at me. Biting her nails, and fidgeting around, she yelled,

"Open it. You don't remember, so open the fucking book you son of a bitch." Seeing her so passionate about this book, had a nigga curious to see what was inside it. Opening it, I saw ultra sounds on each page, with her name on all of them from various months and years. The last page threw me for a loop when I saw a picture of what appeared to be a premature baby.

"What is all of this?" I asked her.

"Your fucking babies." She said.

"Man get the fuck out of here with that bullshit. I slipped up with you one time, and yeah I told you to dead that shit because a nigga wasn't ready for kids and definitely didn't want kids with you," I said.

"But you wanted that ugly ass bastard ass baby with Tommie," she yelled. Clinching my jaw, I had to mentally count down in my head, to keep from killing this bitch.

"If I was you, I would think very carefully about the next words that come out of your mouth. The plans I have for your ass don't include death, but if you let some dumb shit like that come out of your mouth again; if you even so much as mention my daughter one more fucking time, I'll chop your body up into little fucking pieces," I barked.

"I don't give a fuck what your plans include. I made sure all roads lead back to you with everything, not just Henry's death. A death I singled handled masterminded, and was the one to put the battery in his mom's back that you was out to kill her son. And, I even have stuff in motion for if you kill me, sort of my very own insurance policy. It's enough information on you, that you will never see the light of day," she said with an evil grin on her face. "You not smart as you think. So go ahead, pull the trigger. You won't be out of jail long enough to watch the child you love grow up. But if I can't watch my baby grow up, then you won't either. You say you made me have an abortion, but I've been poking holes in your condoms for years. All those ultrasounds are from times I got pregnant and miscarried with each of them. The last time, the time you knew about and made me get an abortion, I didn't. I kept the baby, well until I had a miscarriage at five months. I did everything right to ensure a healthy pregnancy, but still I had a miscarriage. Do you know what it feels like to have to push out a baby that you had already named, knew the sex of, and loved unconditionally? Do you?" She screamed.

"Nope and I hope my girl never has to experience that shit again. I feel bad you went through that shit, real talk ma. However, it ain't a nigga fault that your uterus can't carry full term. You should have stopped after the first two. That damn book is full of ultra sounds, so you did that dumb shit to yourself. If any one of them kids would have lived, I would have one hundred percent took care of mines. I would have probably killed your stupid ass for pulling that bullshit, but I would never be a deadbeat. That shit ain't in me, so don't fucking blame me for the hurt and pain you experiencing," I said.

"Fuck you," she screamed charging at me full force swinging on me. The first lick caught a nigga off guard, but the next time she went to hit me, I twisted her arm behind her back and head butted her ass. Her nose instantly started bleeding as I pushed her down. Turning my back to grab her some napkins off the table, I felt a stinging feeling in my side. Quickly turning back around, I noticed the bitch had stabbed me. Hitting her in the face about four times, I then pulled the small blade out my side and dropped it on the floor. Sitting down on the couch, my breathing picked up as I applied pressure to the wound. Ain't this bout a bitch, nigga done let this hoe stab my ass. That's crazy that the only person to shoot and stab me was this bitch. The stab wound wasn't that deep, so I didn't feel like I was dying or anything, I was just mad I let the shit happen. *Tommie is going to kill my ass when she sees this blood.* Sitting up and spitting out blood, she said,

"That's all you got bitch?" Laughing at her, I said,

"You want a nigga to kill you, but I'm not. Naw that ain't all I got though, you gone love the rest. See once I saw you tailing me that day, I knew you had to have something to do with everything going on. The lips being sent to my house, and all that extra shit. So, I started thinking back to what all you knew bout a nigga to try and calculate your next move. Then, it hit me. I knew you would eventually try and hit my stash house, so I moved all my money and set a trap. You see everything you touched, from the break in, to when y'all dumb asses robbed the bodies has your finger prints on it. I mean I bet Dom's ass $1000 y'all wouldn't search the pockets for money. But, sure enough while passing a blunt back and forth, we watched y'all asses run all them pockets. The only finger prints on the house and bodies are you and Kenneth. I also had a professional forged confession letter sent over to the pigs detailing how you set me up, and you killed those men in a crime of passion because you couldn't have me," I said. Yeah I know a nigga don't fuck with the pigs, and I could have just killed the hoe and got it over with. But, like she pointed out, I'm tryna see both my kids grow up. No matter how many pigs or Feds I pay off, that case would still somehow float to the service. This way a nigga cleared of all charges. Begins, a bullet is too good for her. I'm sure that was her exit plan this entire time. Joke was on her though, because she was not only about to do fed time, but I had a long list of inmates on payroll in that bitch ready to make her life hell.

"You lying, you don't even like the police," she said laughing until she heard sirens. Right on time.

"I may do a lot of things to females lil' momma, but lying to them has never been one. I also tipped the cops off to where you were staying. Since I'm in a giving mood, I'll leave you this," I said taking another gun from behind me.

"I thought you said you wasn't gone kill me?" She said.

"I'm not, you can do the honors yourself though," I said as I got up to make my exit. I wasn't worried about the bitch trying to shoot me in the back, so I didn't even bother walking backwards. I slipped back out the same way I got in. I was halfway to my car before I heard her yelling,

"Fuck you Ghost! Son of a bitch!" I forgot to tell her that the gun didn't have any bullets in it. But, it felt good to get the last laugh.

EPILOGUE

TOMMIE

I found love in you
And I've learned to love me too
Never have I felt that I could be all that you see

Carmen Lashay

As my dad walked me down the aisle to Major *"Why I Love You,"* I couldn't help but tear up as I glanced around the wedding venue out at the sea of faces. The building was jam- packed with all of our closest family and friends here to witness this important milestone in our lives. I was extremely happy my mom got to attend my wedding, because I don't know what I would have done had she not gotten to come, The closer I got to Landon, the harder it was to keep the tears at bay. Today, I was marrying a man I couldn't have dreamed up if I tried. A very loving, goofy, and spontaneous man. A man that was not only my partner in crime, baby daddy, king, superman, and protector, he was also my best friend. He was always there when I need him to be, even if I didn't ask him to be. A man that loved me past the hurt and pain. Who saw more in me at a time when I didn't even see it in myself, and who was my eyes when I couldn't see and voice when I couldn't speak. Any doubts I had in the back instantly left the minute I laid eyes on Landon. I loved this man more than life itself. I didn't love him because he saved me from a life of hell with Rodney. I loved him because he was patient enough to actually show me what real love really was. It was more than social media made it out to be. Real love watching wearing matching clothes yelling relationship goals. Real love wasn't always sugar and spice and everything nice. Real love was being there through the good and the bad, through weight gain and weight loss. Real love was being brutally honest with your partner no matter what, because if you can't be honest with one another, then really what are you doing? Real love can't be turnt on and off like a faucet. You can't love someone today, and another tomorrow. Real love is going through some things in order to grow through some things. Real love isn't having materialistic things. Real love is pure, it's patient, it's kind, and it's unique. That's what I felt as I stood before God, said my vows, exchanged rings, and uttered the two words that would change my life forever, "I Do."

Looking around at my reception at everyone, I couldn't help but to feel overjoyed. This journey had been rocky for everyone managed to come out on top. Me and Landon are in a very good place in our lives. Menace and his new girlfriend seem to really be in love, and even Jasmine has accepted her. Kenyatta and Kenya are officially working for Landon, and even relocated to the area. As for Dom and Jasmine, well stay tuned because I'll let them tell their own story coming next up. Their dynamic story couldn't be summed up in a few words. It needed its own series. I will say though, we all found love in our own way. It really is all fair in Love and Hennessy.

THE END....SIKE it ain't over yet. Keep reading. No for real, keep reading. The book isn't over yet y'all...

EPILOGUE RELOADED

SIX MONTHS LATER….

GHOST I hope y'all didn't think we forgot about Rodney's ass now, did y'all? The twins told me before they killed Chelsea, that she put them up on game about Rodney thinking that would save her life. Bitch just didn't know how to stop fucking running her mouth snitching. Her ass been waiting to tell all she know, that's why she dead now. She told them how she brought him back to a house he had ducked off. After they killed her, they followed her directions that lead back to the place, and went inside. It was empty of course, but guess who left her bible behind? You guessed it, dear ole Aunt Carol. So she not only knew her son was alive, but she helped him escape. I would think long and hard on how I would deal with her, right now, I had this nigga bloody and beaten tied to a chair. It wasn't easy getting his ass here. As a matter of fact, his ass put up a huge fight, so I give him that. He definitely redeemed himself from last time. Nigga must was in the gym day and night hitting iron, and practicing. I think deep down inside, he knew one day I was coming for his ass. Or, he thought he was coming for me. Either way, it's time to eat or be eaten.

"Damn nigga, you still alive? Nigga got nine lives like a cat or some shit," Dom said walking through the door. Rodney had been tied up in the room going on a few days, being beaten and tortured daily, yet he still was alive. I was done playing with his ass today though. I was making sure he was dead this time.

"Because I'm built for this shit, y'all niggas couldn't kill me even if you tried to kill me. So let's gone get this shit over with because a nigga got shit to do," he said as if unfazed by us.

"Whatever you got to do won't get done in this lifetime, yo ass not walking out this bitch this time," I said. He didn't even look bothered as he said,

"I can't die," he said right before we all heard a gun going off.

POW! POW! POW! POW!

As his body jerked from all the bullets entering his body, I saw Tommie's ass walking up holding a gun looking sexy as hell. She had already shook back after giving birth to our son.

"You dying today," she said as her chest heaved up and down as she just stared at him. I knew she needed this closure to put this part of her life behind her. Walking closer to him, she let off a few more shots into his face and head, then looked up at me and said,

"Just making sure he stays dead this time," she says shrugging her shoulders. Running over to the body, Dom looked down at Rodney and said,

"Damn bruh. Nigga, yo head is literally hanging off ya body. She fucked you up. Yo ass is dead today," he said laughing. Walking over to me, Tommie planted a big kiss on my lips and said,

"Let's go home zaddy."

The End

Interested in becoming a part of the Treasured Publications family? Submit manuscripts to Info@Treasuredpub.com Like us on Facebook: Treasured Publications

Be sure to text **Treasured** to **444999** To subscribe to our Mailing List. Never miss a release or contest again!

CPSIA information can be obtained
at www.ICGtesting.com
Printed in the USA
LVHW081519160520
655790LV00007B/162

9 781985 274945